The Orangutan Rescue Gang

by Joyce Major

First published in the United States in 2019 by Alegro Publishing
Copyright © Joyce Major, 2019

Library of Congress Control Number: 2019902240
ISBN: 978 0 578 43831 3 print
ISBN: 978 0 578 43833 7 eBook
10 9 8 7 6 5 4 3 2 1

Alegro Publishing
Seattle, WA

Editor: Ann Creel
Copy Editor: Kathleen Glica
Design: Steve Mead
Cover design: Steve Mead

All design elements from Shutterstock.
Printed in the USA

Acknowledgements

There is a powerful force unleashed when young people
resolve to make a change.

— Jane Goodall

Also by Joyce Major

Smiling at the World

For all those who stand up for what they believe
in and for my family

CHAPTER 1

THE ADVENTURE BEGINS

As far as I can figure, today is like every other day here in Medan, Sumatra: hot sticky air, crowded to the max, honks and screeches. Some guy on a scooter speeding through the narrow pathway, swerving around vegetables piled on the ground, dodging slow shoppers and heading right at me? What? With a yelp, I dodged him. Good thing I play soccer, I thought. My nose sniffed around like a bunny or maybe a bloodhound as the extra hot sun ratcheted up the smell of dead, shiny, silvery fish laid out in rows across long tables at this open-air market. Rising to my tiptoes, straining to see above or between the crowds, I scanned the area looking for anything familiar. *Home.* I'd never been anywhere like this before. It was as if Dad and I were dropped onto a movie set swarming with people. As heat rose in waves off the street, sweat dripped off my face. This place was totally overwhelming.

Let me say right off, moving to Sumatra, Indonesia, was not my idea. Where is Indonesia you say? Try over 8,000 miles from Seattle, which is one third of the way around the whole world, in the middle of the Indian Ocean! It's an island. I mean, would you want to leave home, all your friends and miss sleeping late every single day of summer vacation? Not me. I'd miss the Sounders Soccer Youth Camp and swimming in Lake Washington. Then like every summer of my life, I was certain that my parents would finally say yes to getting a dog. My grades were good enough and I made my bed every day. Well, almost every day.

I'm still trying to figure out how Dad tricked me into coming with him. But here I am, both feet on the ground, jostling through the crowd, scrunched between strangers, weaving through a market that looks nothing like Pike Place Market back home. We're supposed to buy groceries except that none of these fruits or vegetables looked familiar except for the bananas.

"Gross! See that? You'll never catch me eating chicken here! Too gross!" Dead chickens dangled upside down hanging by thick yellow rope tied to their stiff, ugly, red feet. They had fluffy brownish feathers and red crowns. Big revolting black flies with red eyes crawled all around their bodies, in and out of their sunken, glazed, dead eyes.

Dad tousled my hair, sending my crazy curls even farther out than normal. When I grinned up at him, he cracked a smile. "Remember, we're here to learn first-hand about this culture," he told me.

Rolling my eyes, I sighed. "Whatever. It's crazy hot," I said, wiping my forehead with the back of my hand. "I'm boiling in people stew."

Dad replied with not a word. Zippo, zero, zilch.

I poked him on the arm. "Hey!" Poke. Poke. "Dad?" Poke. "You in there?"

Shaking his head, he grinned at me like string held up the corners of his mouth. "What honey?"

"Nothing." Dad didn't seem too interested in me or even worried about me wandering around in a new country.

But then my eye caught something strange. It looked like some kind of monkey. Screeching to a halt, I yanked on Dad's hand. "STOP! Look over there. A little baby animal. Let's go see him," I said.

"He's wild, Jaylynn. We can't go up to strange wild animals in a foreign country. Don't forget, even dogs bite strangers."

"But Dad, look how sad he is. We have to go see him. Come on..."

Stretching out, I yanked on Dad's arm, sure that I could make him stop but he wasn't having any of it. Was I ready to give up? Never. As Dad got distracted, I slipped away and sprinted over to have a closer look. Shoulders hunched, and head downcast, he looked like a little statue of gloom. The poster child for misery, fastened to a big, heavy, gorilla-sized chain, surrounded by barren dirt, adorable, with reddish hair, almost the same color as mine. What went so sour in his life to be left outside, unprotected, with nowhere to hide? Where was his mom? The hot sun beat down on him relentlessly.

Grinning to myself, crouching low, creeping closer until finally I tiptoed right up to him. Using my softest, gentlest, sugary voice like talking to my baby cousin, Penelope, I spoke to him and he didn't run away. He stared right into my eyes as I gasped and held my breath. We looked at each other like we were the only two things on earth. Everything around us disappeared. No sounds. No smells. Magic.

"Hello there, little guy. How ya doing? Never seen a monkey up close before, well, maybe at the zoo. You're beautiful," I cooed.

I shook my head, rolling my eyes and reminded myself that his chances of understanding me weren't any better than Uncle Dan's dog. But then, his coal black eyes were unwavering and seemingly demanding of my attention. I thought, why not?

"My name is Jaylynn. I'm eleven, almost twelve."

He watched me, his eyes pinned to mine like he understood. Squatting close enough to touch his back, I slowly reached my hand out, gradually, with no jerky movements, closer and closer and my fingers stretched out almost close enough to touch him, a few inches more, almost there...

And then BAM! A giant vice flew down and clamped onto my hand, drawing it back and tipping me onto my bottom, scaring the poor monkey away. I yanked, tugged, wiggled to escape but he had me. Turning, fist up, ready to fight. "DAD?"

"WHAT DID I TELL YOU YOUNG LADY! HE'S WILD!" Dad looked like a volcano ready to blow. "YOU CAN'T GO UP TO STRANGE WILD ANIMALS IN A FOREIGN COUNTRY. DON'T FORGET THAT EVEN DOGS BITE STRANGERS. YOU MUST LISTEN TO ME. DO YOU UNDERSTAND? NO MONKEYS!"

Dad took my hand firmly but as we walked away, I stared back certain that the monkey's eyes locked onto mine. He needed me, I could tell. I had to find a way to get back there. No matter what Dad said. Little did I know that with that brief encounter, my first great adventure had begun.

"After our walk, we'll meet our new cook, Gita, and her son, Zaqi. He's eleven like you. Should be great to have the benefit of a new friend from Sumatra. I arranged for them to live in the downstairs apartment at our new house to make it easier for all of us."

"Say what? I'm not sure I want to live with some random boy, Dad." I stood frozen, glaring at Dad, lost in a muddle of irritation.

Dad replied with not a word. Zippo, zero, zilch.

I poked him on the arm. "Hey." Poke. Poke. "Dad?" Poke. "You in there?" Lately Dad flew in and out of our conversations as if his brain took an elevator past our floor. I glanced up at Dad, who was preoccupied in another daydream. Mom used to tease him about all his daydreaming, but he said it gave him his best ideas.

Certain I could sneak off to find the monkey and return before he even missed me, I slipped away, darting between people like a forward dribbling toward goal. I took a couple of turns and stopped, certain I'd found the right spot but as I spun around... no monkey. Where was he? Shaking my head, I looked around some more but no luck, no monkey.

Guessing I'd better get back to Dad before he missed me, I backtracked, but he wasn't standing at the butcher shop anymore. With his blonde hair, I figured he'd be easy to spot in the sea of dark hair, but no Dad. I stood on my tiptoes wishing I was taller, scanning the crowded aisles and telling myself not to panic. My red hair would be easy for him to spot. Right? "Dad? Dad, where are you? DAD!" I shouted. Where could he be? "DAD!"

My cheeks went cold as the blood drained from my face. My knees turned to jelly, my hands shook, my lower lip quivered, I was a total mess, which meant tears were coming next. Lost? No Dad anywhere. I was alone. In Sumatra?

I searched for a spot to stand and wait, to hug a tree like they taught us in camp, but the whoosh of the crowd pushed me forward like I was riding a strong current on the Snoqualmie River back home. I put my arms up, flailing around to signal for help, and finally, managed to edge my way out of the flow of the crowd.

Straining to listen for Dad's familiar voice over the blare of motorcycles and people shouting in different languages, the reality of being lost hit me hard. My stomach hurt like a monster was punching from the inside out. Did I even have our address? I had no money and no phone either. Only my Hazel Valley School ID, like that was going to help. *What could I do now? Just don't panic. But nobody even speaks English here. Stay calm. Dad will find me... Or will I be lost here forever?*

This whole mess was my own dumb fault. What was I thinking? Why did I always make bad choices? What made me think for one second that I could go see the monkey and Dad would never even miss me? Boy, was I wrong. Not a clever idea at all, to sneak away and this time I'd really blown it. What a loser. Too short to spot in the crowd, I kept spinning around. For a few seconds, I closed my eyes hoping that when I opened them, Dad would appear like magic. Dad? I'm here. Find me. Please.

Why did we move to this dumb city anyway? It was

all Mom's fault, for sure. She accepted her dream job in Washington, D.C. and blathered on endlessly about her once-in-a-lifetime opportunity to work as lead scientist for the climate change agency. For me, her dream job meant no more Mom and it meant tearing our family apart till we landed in faraway places.

To make matters worse, as it turned out, her move was only the half of it. Her scent barely vanished from the house, when Dad announced another bigger, more radical change—his new job with an oil company. It hurled us across the ocean to Indonesia, setting me down here, standing all alone in Sumatra. Lost and desperate. My throat felt like a hand was strangling me, stealing my air, muffling my voice.

But then I turned around and there he was…the monkey!

Chapter 2

Day One

A little cheer squeaked out of my mouth. From my spot, as if peering through binoculars, I scrutinized him—observing, examining, and scoping out the area around him like an undercover cop. Is there someone here to take care of him?

When I tiptoed up to him, that little monkey gazed right into my eyes and all the way to my heart. Thing was, being this close didn't scare me a bit. I figured he'd be afraid and run for it, but he stayed.

I couldn't find my breath. His sad eyes blinked slowly, like human eyes, studying me. His lips parted silently. Everything around us disappeared. We looked at each other like no one else in the world existed. Rejoicing. I wanted to say "thank you" but I merely gawked, smitten with love at first sight. My breathing slowed, matching the little monkey's breath. Connection. Understanding. Magic.

"I am lost. Definitely all alone," I said softly. "Dad missed me, back there, somewhere." I pointed behind me. But my worries left, and calm filled me as I stared into the little monkey's mournful black eyes. "What a beauty. Looks like you apply highlighter eye shadow around your eyes and mouth. Thin, narrow eyebrows like you pluck them and your skin looks like chocolate." A grin flashed across my face.

"Lucky you, no freckles. See all my gingerbread dots? Freckles everywhere. Your jaw looks like you're always blowing up your cheeks with air. Like this." I blew up my cheeks with air. "See?"

"My nose must look giant compared to yours." As I moved my finger around the tip of my nose, he observed carefully as if taking in the details. "See, yours is like mostly nostril holes. Dude, your fur looks more like wiry hair like mine but not curly." I turned my hands up and over. "See, no hair, like yours. I wonder why you stare at me so intently. Glad you're not afraid. You're like the best thing that's happened to me since I landed in Sumatra. Wonder when Dad will find me..."

He gazed into my eyes, asking me something, but what? I remembered that look from Uncle Dan's dog when he needed a scratch behind the ears.

At that instant, some feeling in my gut tickled me, something odd and something new. "OMG, I'm wigging out. This might sound dumb, but I can almost hear you if my head quiets down. Am I cracking up?" Curious about the weird sensation, I went silent. Sitting together in the mustard-colored dirt, perfectly content to wait for his reply. Looking back at that moment, guess I didn't know enough to suspect the wild adventure sneaking up on my life.

"Why isn't your mother here?"

The baby monkey looked like he wanted to answer.

His face folded into sadness. Even without words, he communicated with me.

"You poor thing. No mom to protect you. I know that one. You can barely hold your head up with that shackle around your tiny neck. Someone tied you up with a gorilla chain that weighs more than you. Aren't you scared?" I asked. "I'm freaked out." Looking at him, I knew he was petrified, too. "We're a pair. You lost your mom and I can't find Dad."

Suddenly, feeling scared and alone and stupid for leaving Dad's side, I rolled my eyes around hoping to beat back tears, but they dropped one by one. The monkey gazed deeper into my eyes, watching my teardrops fall. His head tilted to one side, never shifting his eyes off mine.

"How can I find Dad?" I turned my head to scout for Dad but only saw strangers. My head collapsed into my hands, and the tears returned. I tried holding my breath to stop, but a sob escaped. So, embarrassed and crying in front of a little monkey. I cried way too much.

But when I lifted my head, the little monkey wasn't mad at all. "Looking at your gentle eyes and sweet face, I want to hug you except you're not a stuffed animal. Maybe you're even dangerous? No, not dangerous. The longer I look at you, the less alone I feel." My breathing slowed, and my tears stopped falling.

Just then, a guy on a motorcycle roared down the street, swerving straight at us. The monkey ran to the wall, but I didn't know where to hide and he was coming too fast to move out of the way. "Dad," I screamed, "Help!" My arms wrapped around my head hoping to save my brains from being crushed by a motorcycle as the engine roared. Maybe it would have been smarter to stand up and shout but instead I hunkered down as the smell of gasoline filled my nose. Every muscle in my body tightened when tires screeched on pavement. *Please stop. Don't hit me.* Miraculously, in the nick of time, the motorcycle veered, spraying me with dirt but no contact. The waba waba from my heart beat loudly.

"Phew, close call. You see that? Crazy drivers. Not Seattle." My plan? Keep talking, jabbering away to my new friend until he got brave enough to come back to me. "Anyway, I'm eleven. Think I told you that already. How old are you? Wish I could tell you why I'm here. Not my choice. Guess Dad's idea of a cool adventure was moving here with his new job but look at me now."

My eyes filled with tears again as I looked across the market searching for Dad.

"OMG, how am I going to get home?" I covered my face with my hands, hoping an answer would surface. "Little monkey, you and I'll figure out a solution. Sure, we will." After those words had barely escaped my mouth, he walked back to me, reached out his hand and grabbed my arm. His fingers squeezed tight and made little impressions on my skin. "Dude, now what?"

CHAPTER 3

DAY ONE CONTINUES

Flabbergasted, I grimaced, bracing myself, hoping he wouldn't bite hard, but felt only the warmth of his skin exactly like a human. Each finger precisely like mine, even the creases at the knuckles and his black fingernails shaped like mine.

Still a little bit afraid, I heard Dad's voice in my head warning me to stay away. He'd say that I wasn't using the brains I was born with. He'd tell me I'd be bitten. But what did Dad know and where was he now? Nowhere and I was alone in the market because of his stupid idea to move here. And besides, I wanted this monkey to like me.

I laid my other hand over his hand, which was covered in little wisps of red hair. Gentle, soft and warm. Safe. My new best friend, but something else. "Weird. So, I see or sort of feel green? If I use my eyes, I lose it. Is that some message from you? Awesome. Maybe it's like some kind of telepathy? So, I see rainforest. You see rainforest?"

Tilting my head, I waited for an answer.

"*Phruff*…. what am I expecting?"

But a feeling of moving, swaying green stayed with me.

"You're swaying in your tree and bringing me along? Is that what's happening? It's lush and peaceful and feels so free, like flying."

As I searched his eyes to understand the color, only the unknown appeared. His thin little eyebrows raised as if asking a question and wanting an answer.

"I love floating in your green world. Little monkey, I'd be so scared here without you."

From somewhere in the market, snapping me out of my reverie, came shouting. Words stormed at me like a gust of wind off Puget Sound. "OMG, it's getting closer. Wonder what that's about?" Slowly turning my head toward the noise, I spotted him. A man dressed in a white polo shirt, khaki pants, and baseball cap. He looked like an ordinary person but warrior fierce. His strong strides quickly swallowed up the distance as his feet pounded the dirt. *Yelling? But why?*

"*APA YANG KAMU LAKUKAN?*" he growled. "*KELUAR DARI SINI!*" Shrieking, he waved his clenched fists in the air declaring war. "*BIARKAN ORANGUTAN ITU SENDIRIAN!*" Anger oozed out of every line on his bitter face. Little O ran to hide near the wall. *What was he afraid of?*

"What's happening?" I asked, gulping hard. "What's wrong with him?"

For a minute too long, figuring he was heading somewhere else, I watched. Wrong! In like two seconds, he stood in front of me. Towering over me. Screaming. "*KELUAR DARI SINI!*" He spun towards me then lunged, reaching out to grab me. Absolute terror ran down my spine. I did the only thing I knew. I ran. Flying out of there, bumping into people, not looking back, petrified he'd catch me. Finally, I stopped. My body quivered, my heart pounded so hard I could feel it in my ears, my breath came in jerks. But, even though I knew it was incredibly dumb, I slowly snuck back. Stopping at a corner stand and questioning the wisdom of playing hide-and-go-seek with a maniac, my head inched forward and one eye curled around to spy.

The Maniac Man stood above the baby monkey, yanking hard on his chain, yelling at him. "*ORANGUTAN BODOH! DUDUKLA! AKU HARUS MENYINGKIRKAN ANDA SEKARANG*" he hollered.

What? NO! He pulled the baby orangutan back to the store wall. He hit him—hard. Way too hard.

"Stop. No!" I whispered.

And he hit him again. *How can I stop him?* I watched in horror. When the man planted his hands on his hips and looked in my direction, I quickly ducked for cover, certain he saw me. As still as a statue, barely breathing, I peeked out again.

The man aimed his finger like a gun at the little monkey. "*ORANGUTAN BODOH!*" he roared. He looked all around again with a scowl plastered across his face. Then he walked away.

I wanted to go back there but was that too dangerous? And then, a color filled up my insides. Red. From the monkey? Panic? Panting like a frightened child, trying to calm myself but terror and despair filled my insides. He's telling me something horrible, but what?

Searching my gut, it didn't take long to uncover my own red space. My hollowed out empty spot filled with thorns and prickly things. My stomach tied into knots. Life without Mom. I dredged up how miserable I felt when she left us. How dejected. He showed me his empty spot, without his mom, scared to death and totally unprotected.

I ran back to him, no longer afraid, wanting only to protect the baby monkey who had sent me red. Scanning the area, I kept my eyes peeled for another terror attack from Maniac Man. Bravery was not one of my top ten characteristics, but this little monkey needed me.

Cuddled up next to him, boiling in the heat from the hottest sun ever as each ray of sunlight melted me into perspiration overdrive.

"You miss your mom, right? The way I hear you is so different, but it makes me remember my hole inside. I don't have a mom now, either."

My lips quivered. The hair on the back of my neck stood up as an even stronger sense of his alarm passed through me. A tear fell from my eye. "Mom left me. She's not around anymore. She said her job was important, but I never see her now, like you and your mom. It's almost like she's dead. What happened to your mother?"

Hunched over, popping his lips, his eyes filled with sorrow, the monkey sent me red and I tilted my head in astonishment. "These colors describe your feelings?" The little monkey popped his lips. "That's it. We're like the same. I'm so sorry that he hurt you. He's horrible," I said. Powerless to walk away and abandon him, I sat in the dirt leaning against the wall and rubbed his back. "You hurt, sweet baby?" I said, glancing into his eyes. "But why would he hit you? Maybe it's my fault. Maybe I need to leave you alone."

He raised his eyebrows and tilted his head.

"So, Mom used to rub my back whenever I was afraid. I hope this makes you feel better, too," I suggested. As I rubbed his back, my breathing slowed, a grand sigh escaped my lips, and my eyes gazed off into the distance. "Hey, missing our moms sucks. I feel it in my heart, the Great Empty that nothing can fill, right?"

Then, the empty spot in my heart changed to a new color. Yellow. A big burst of yellow, like the sun filling me with warmth and happiness, filling up my chest like a balloon moving out all the sadness. "Now that means what? Guess if I stopped yakking, I'd understand. Love this way of talking." I sat perfectly still. Didn't say a word. Waited. "Okay, got it. Yellow, hot like the sun, is love, right?" I gazed at that little monkey and he crawled into my lap and lay his head down on my shoulder. My sigh was so deep that his fur was tousled by the breeze. When a gigantic bubble of yellow enveloped me, I smiled my first real smile since landing in Sumatra. Warm. Safe. The baby monkey reached out and held onto my arm as I laid my hand on his. We sat that way for a long time though I skimmed the crowd for Maniac Man, afraid and certain of his return.

"OMG, it's hotter than the blazes here. Even my eyeballs are boiling. Sticky arms, sticky face. Indonesia is nothing like home," I exclaimed.

My mind drifted to cool, green, wet Seattle with the smell of fresh air. *Home*. From somewhere in my brain, I flashed on a word that Maniac Man yelled, something that sounded like *orangutan*.

"That's it! I'm so stupid. Of course, you're not a monkey at all. Jeez…sorry, you're a baby orangutan. And you need a name. Like—Ozzie Orangutan. Or Oscar. But maybe you're a girl. Olivia? I know, Little O for little orangutan."

Looking around, squinting my eyes to see in the distance, listening for Dad's voice calling me, I said, "When Dad finds us, he'll know how to help you. He'll find us any time now." But as I scanned for Dad to rescue me, I also knew that Maniac Man could pop out any minute from anywhere. Nothing to do but wait and hope. "Let's see about talking in colors," I told him. "Green for the forest, red for fear, and yellow for love…"

As I blabbered away, Little O moved his hands from my arm to my head. His little fingers moved through each strand of my hair, like he was looking for bugs and I hoped he didn't find any. Too gross!

"Wow, that's a crazy feeling. Ten little fingers moving through my hair. So light. Right? I've always wanted a dog but like no luck on that one yet. If I had a dog, we'd go for walks and cuddle. He'd protect me. I'd brush him. I'd gaze into his eyes, too. You know about dogs? If you were my pet, I'd take you home, brush your hair, and let you sleep on my bed."

Little O continued grooming my hair.

"Thanks, by the way, for grooming me. It feels good. When I was little, Mom always helped with my wild curly hair. Now I grab it all into a ponytail like this, see?"

Little O, obviously not approving, pulled my hair out of the ponytail.

"Sorry, if I'm talking too much, babbling really. Guess, like, it's the nerves talking. So, lucky you're here to help me. I'd be a total mess without you."

As Little O continued to look for bugs, I relaxed. Having him in my lap, grooming my hair, it all felt perfectly natural like we'd been friends forever. Finally, I stopped jabbering and I quieted, no need for words. Friends don't always need to talk. I groomed his fur hoping with all my might, I wouldn't find any bugs. While peace sunk into my heart, an idea hit me like a coconut falling on my head.

"Little O, you must escape from Maniac Man, get back to the rainforest and the safety of your mom's arms. It's my mission to get that done. The sooner the better."

CHAPTER 4

DAY ONE ENDS

Sitting cross-legged in the dirt for what seemed like hours, the red-hot sun broiled my brains like crisp bacon. Scorching hot with a sunburn forming on my arms, perspiration was racing down my temples and neck, plastering my t-shirt to my body like a wet rag.

Little O wasn't sweating at all but had a lot of curiosity about mine because he reached his little hand over to my cheek and gently wiped at a big mess of moisture dripping down my face. He rubbed it between his thumb and finger like a science experiment. Finally, he tasted it. Beyond embarrassed, I lowered my head in my hands.

"Ah, Little O, um, I'm not sure you should taste that. Too gross."

Little O suddenly seemed unable to understand me. That's when he plunked his other finger into his mouth smacking his lips together like a famous chef on *Taste*. Taking his tongue and running it along his lips, he tilted his head to the side as if, for a moment, judging.

"You eat salty foods in the jungle?" I asked. Giggles escaped as I watched him. He nodded his head slowly as if in praise. Too funny. Then lifting his hand, he gently dragged it across my other cheek wiping away the wetness.

After that, I threw my head back laughing. "Little O, I can't believe you're licking my sweat. I love you so much but that's disgusting. Dripping perspiration isn't considered edible back home. And you're totally ignoring me. Please stop."

But Little O paid no attention, placing each finger into his mouth, smacking his lips together as if sampling chocolate pudding! So, I had no choice, I tilted my head down, grabbed the bottom of my t-shirt, and wiped away all traces of perspiration from my face. "Little O, I love you!"

Little O seemed a bit miffed at what I'd done to his treat.

"I'll try to find something else for you to drink," I said. From our spot low on the ground, I saw food stands but none with any water bottles and I had zero money. "Little O, I'm going into that store for water. I'll be right back."

Little O smacked his lips together, hard and fast, making a sound like "poppoppoppoppoppop."

"What's wrong? You're frightened?" I asked. "I'll be right back. I promise."

Still Little O smacked his lips together and sent me red. What was he afraid of? Maybe he thought I was leaving him forever.

"Little O don't be afraid. I'm getting us water and then we can cuddle. I won't leave you."

Walking into the store, I hesitated for a moment trying to figure out what was scaring

Little O. What made him afraid? Thinking of Maniac

Man, I clenched my fist. Maybe I should have brought a stick inside for extra safety. *Jaylynn, relax, it's a store and you need water.* I hoped someone spoke English. My eyes slowly adjusted to the dim lights inside, the aisles barely wide enough for one person. The shelves were piled sky high to the ceiling with strange things. An icy shiver snaked along my spine, but I ignored it and looked around for bottles of water. From the back of the store I heard, *"Selamat siang apa kabar?"*

Upon hearing that voice, a tremor shook throughout my body like a small earthquake. That voice sounded like… No, couldn't be but then the hair rose on the back of my neck. *Who was that? Why am I shaking? Maniac Man?* I tried to speak but nothing came out. Finally, I sputtered, "Water, do you have any water?"

From the rear of the store, "Water? *Aix? Ya.*"

Warily, ignoring my intuition I walked toward the back of the store, toward the voice that sounded eerily familiar. When I rounded the aisle, I froze. The sight of the man standing before me made my skin crawl. Maniac Man! Automatically, my fists clenched, and I backed away slowly heading toward the door. Maybe I could get out before he recognized me or heard my heart beating like a timpani drum. I scanned the shelves for anything to use as a weapon. One slow step at a time. *Don't panic. Back away slowly. A predator attacks their prey when they run. I think I learned that in school.* My heart throbbed loudly. One instant later Maniac Man recognized me, and then everything happened at once.

"AKU PUNYA KAMU SEKARANG." he yelled.

Jumping from behind the counter, he came after me. I stood frozen in fear, as if my feet were cast in cement as Maniac Man charged me. Run!

Panicked, I spun around to escape. I had to get away. But my foot slipped crashing me to the ground. Scrambling to get up, he lurched after me, took hold of my wrist and squeezed it tight in a death grip. "Help! Help!" I screamed.

"Aku punya kamu sekarang. Apa yang kamu lakukan? Aku akan memanggil polisi?"

Every swear word I knew but never said until now came flying out of my mouth. His fingers bore into my wrist, and I struggled to free myself from his grip. My skin burned from his grasp. I had to escape before something bad happened and maybe Dad would never find me here. What if he hit me like Little O? Tied me up? Or worse. I yelled louder digging my heels into the floor as he dragged me towards the back of the store.

But he had an iron grip. How could I get away? Up to me to save myself. Who knows what he would do to me? But then I remembered how he beat Little O and my fear disappeared. Anger replaced it. In the middle of a tug-of-war with my own body, I flashed on the one way out of this mess. My legs tensed ready for action. Newfound strength burned through my body. Without thinking, I rolled to my side, got my feet under me and stood up. Now to get rid of this monster. If I remembered correctly and moved with confidence. Just like before a free kick, I counted. *One, two, three!*

Drawing back my right leg, the one I used to shoot for goal, I inhaled deeply. Then exhaling hard, I snapped my foot around and out, fast and hard. I kicked Maniac Man brutally. Landed that kick smack dab in his privates! BAM! As hard as I could. It worked! He howled like a wounded wolf doubling over in pain, roaring in agony. His fist opened, releasing my wrist. *You're free! Run!* But my knees were too wobbly to move, scared to death, trembling. I wanted to curl up in a corner and cry. *Run Jaylynn. Run!* I staggered out of the store. Tears flying from my eyes, I looked around not knowing where to hide. *Where is it safe? Back by Little O? Where's Dad?* A groan from Maniac Man, snapped me out of my trance. Jetting away from that store faster than ever, I ran wild in the opposite direction not looking back and silently thanking Mom for the self-defense class.

Before long I stopped—winded and distraught—my body shaking. No one here to protect me. Mom always described me as capable and smart, but she had that all wrong. My head sank into the quicksand of helplessness. Lost. All alone. No Dad to protect me. Where could I go?

And then waves of yellow washed over me. No doubt about it. Little O sent me a message loud and clear. Love. My first friend in Indonesia, an orangutan. Remembering my important new job, what I wanted now more than ever, and the last thing I expected when we moved to Sumatra: Get Little O away from Maniac Man. No more beatings. Get Little O back to the rainforest. I'm the one to do it!

My eyes narrowed like a hunter looking for water and spotting another store. I entered cautiously. Immediately, a man with a good-natured face and gray hair, wearing a printed shirt and khaki pants greeted me with a smile that crinkled the wrinkles around his eyes.

"*Ibu? Ayah?*" he said looking around me.

Of course, I shrugged not understanding. Holding an imaginary water bottle to my mouth, pointing to my tongue, panting like a dog. He grinned at me like my antics amused him and nodded. "*Ya. Ya. Aix.*" He pointed to a water bottle. "*Ya?*"

Before I took it, I pulled my empty pockets inside out to show him and held out my empty hands hoping that he understood, no money. "*Ya. Ya. Tidak ada masalah.*" He waved both hands at me, smiling.

"Thank you, bye bye." After that, I smiled wishing I could say 'thank you' in his language. Happy to be given water with a smile, I left the store in a few quick, light steps.

He waved back at me beaming, "*Kembali ke sini jika anda memerlukan bantuan.*"

Feeling much better, I wound my way back to Little O, very aware of my surroundings and keeping my distance from the store entrance, my eyes peeled for Maniac Man. Meanwhile, I looked around for a rock or a stick. He better stay inside the store but more than anything, I wished that I'd spot Dad.

Little O bobbed his head up and down when he spotted me. "*Meep…meep…meep.*" A wave of yellow washed over me. He climbed onto my lap, holding my shoulders with his hands and resting his head on my chest. "Hey, Little O, you ever see a water bottle before? Here's how you drink from them." Chugging down the water, I realized how thirsty I was and wanted to gulp it all down at once, but Little O gazed up at me with his beautiful eyes. "Yes, yes, yes. Give the bottle a try. It's all yours."

Little O grabbed the bottle and drank the rest in a couple of swallows. Afterwards he wrapped himself around me and cuddled into my chest. Orangutan love. Thunderstruck by his affection, I rubbed his back while he hummed sweet little sounds of contentment.

Absorbed in daydreams, I fantasized about living with Little O. He could sleep with me wrapped up in yellow. A way better pet than a dog, if only Dad would let me. Hold up! Smacking myself on the forehead, I was such a yoyo. That was not my mission.

CHAPTER 5

DAY ONE ENDS

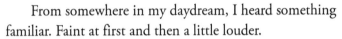

From somewhere in my daydream, I heard something familiar. Faint at first and then a little louder.

"Jaylynn. Jaylynn." Louder... then, moving closer... "JAYLYNN."

"Yes, Dad," I answered quietly, not believing what I'd heard. Not wanting to disturb Little O all snuggled in my lap, I twirled my head around. "DAD!" I shouted. "Little O, I need to run. It's Dad."

I gently eased Little O off my lap, hating to disturb him. He gazed at me longingly, not understanding at all. Anxious to reach Dad, my head turned away and in a flash, I popped straight up running toward him, but away from Little O.

I hopped and jumped and threw my arms in the air, dodging around people, jostling everyone. Colliding recklessly into him, then jumping into his arms and squeezing him with all my might, sniffing his familiar scent. Closing my eyes, I snuggled into his neck, ecstatic. "Dad, Dad, am I glad to see you!"

"Not half as glad as I am to see you." Holding my face

between his hands, he gazed into my eyes. "Losing you terrified me," he told me.

"Dad, I went a little ways away and when I came back, I couldn't see you," I replied. "OMG, terrified? Try petrified!"

"I had no idea where you disappeared, sweetheart. If anything had happened to you... You stayed safe?" he asked.

"Yes. Because of Little O, the baby orangutan over there. I thought you'd never find me. Under no circumstances can you ever lose me again. Promise?"

"Of course, of course, I'm so sorry this happened, Jaylynn. Well, it's been quite a first day. You must be tired, honey. Maybe it's time to head back." He wrapped me up in a big bear hug. Melting into the safety of Dad's arms, I let out a long sigh of relief but then a shower of red swept over me. Little O's fear rained in sheets as I clung to Dad.

"But what about my friend, Little O? I can't abandon him. He's the reason I survived, and I promised him that we'd help him. Please Dad." I looked up into his eyes with the most mournful gaze I could muster. He was right about being exhausted but still, a promise was a promise. My mission was to rescue him.

"Honey, how about if we go home, get some sleep and then come back, spend time with, what do you call him? Little O?"

I rubbed my eyes certain a sack of bricks had fallen on top of me. "Right... I'm like, really pooped out."

"Maybe we'd be smart to get some sleep." Then Dad wrapped his arm around me and my head lowered to his shoulder. My whole body wanted to collapse.

"But we're coming back. That's for sure. Right?"

Dad rubbed my back and smiled gently. "Of course, honey."

Turning back to Little O, I waved goodbye and sent him a balloon of yellow, but I felt like a traitor leaving my best friend behind. And the worst part? Little O was silent. Was I sending the wrong color? I had to let him know that I was sticking to my pledge, that I would come back, but there just weren't enough colors. Abandoning my friend, we walked out into the maze of noisy, jam-packed city streets.

Passing new and old buildings that looked completely different from home, through neighborhoods with palm trees, until finally we reached the security gates of our quiet, perfectly groomed housing project surrounded by tall, wrought iron fencing. Our house—painted white with brown trim—looked modern and kind of stately with a balcony on the second floor. A big palm tree out front even had green coconuts way up high.

Once inside, I bolted upstairs straight to my bedroom. My too white bedroom, with its white bedspread, white dresser, white nightstand, and white rug on the bare floor. Climbing over all the unopened boxes stacked in piles, not bothered by the mess, I flopped onto my bed.

Everything in my life looked like my room—topsy-turvy. I jumped out of bed and rifled through my unpacked suitcases looking for my favorite jammies, the ones with holes in the elbows and knees. I chucked the whole shebang out on the floor. There they were. When I picked them up, I inhaled deeply to sniff a trace of home. Home in Seattle.

Then, I picked up mom's photo, clutching it in both hands. "You agreed to work far away in Washington, D.C., leaving me without a mom and now I need your help. I've stumbled upon a baby orangutan and I must save him but what do I know about rescuing orangutans?"

A knock at the door interrupted my gloomy storm.

"Hi, honey. *Phew...* So many boxes. Tomorrow you'll unpack and get organized but right now, sleep is important to help with jet lag. It's 14 hours difference you know, the middle of the night back home. Jaylynn, are you all right?

"Tired" I whispered, mesmerized by the ceiling fan, not able to look him straight in the eyes and lie.

"I've been reviewing your crazy day. So sorry that I messed up and left you unprotected. I'm proud of you. In a tough situation, you survived by hugging a tree, staying in the same spot and doing all the right things."

I nodded like I agreed but still clung to my despair.

"What a tough start! I can't imagine your panic not knowing how to find me or speak the language," he added. His eyes softened. "You landed in a new country; you got lost in a foreign market and parked yourself next to a baby monkey till I found you!"

"First, you know it's an orangutan, Dad. And I felt like one of those dead chickens hanging from a rope like we saw at the market."

"I'm so sorry, Jaylynn. I'll get you a cell phone in the morning and we'll always stay connected. Believe me, never again will I lose you. You've been through a lot, honey."

"But finding Little O kept me safe. Sitting with him saved me. Kept me from all out panic. We helped each other, we were in it together, but now I get to be home safe with you and he's still there all alone. I'm so worried about him."

"Well, he's a very cute baby animal, that's certain, and I'm grateful that he helped you through your ordeal. Let's both get some sleep and catch up to jet lag."

Dad leaned over, gave me one of his head pats and smiled. "Yes, Jaylynn. Now tuck yourself in for a well-deserved rest. Love you."

"Love you too. And you know, we're going back to the market to see Little O."

CHAPTER 6

DAY TWO BEGINS

The next morning, I zoomed down the stairs, fired up and ready to save Little O, but screeched on the brakes when I saw Dad sitting at a table with an unfamiliar woman and a kid.

"Well, there you are. Jaylynn, now that you're rested, let me introduce you to Gita, our new cook and house helper."

Honestly, I had no interest in meeting anyone and dropped my head down looking at the floor.

"*Selamat siang*, Missy Jaylynn." Gita smiled. When I shot her a hasty "hello" I noticed her large kind dark eyes with super long eyelashes, tiny nose and that she was about Mom's height but petite with shiny black hair pulled back in a tight ponytail, with skin the color of cinnamon. Pretty. Since she walked over to shake my hand, I shook it but wished that I could have hid myself entirely.

Dad continued the introductions. "Honey, this is Zaqi, her son, and your new friend."

Curious about this Zaqi kid, I peeked out of the corner of my eye for a split second and sized him up fast. He was wiry, thin as a reed, and a little taller than me, which wasn't hard. He had crow black hair, straight as silk that almost covered his eyes and molasses-colored skin. Then there was me: head down, not interested in friendship.

Gita laid her arm affectionately around Zaqi and whispered in his ear. With his eyes focused on the floor, a few words sputtered out of his mouth. "Good morning to you, Missy Jaylynn."

Well, at least we had that in common. Totally uncomfortable.

"So, Dad, let's get going to the market. You need to meet my new friend, the baby orangutan, who helped me the whole time I was alone," I replied.

"Friend? You call that creature a friend?" Dad's face filled with astonishment.

Zaqi lifted his gaze from the ground. "You mean wild animal? You friends?"

Jerking my head up and down like a bobble head doll, I yelled, "YES! Can you believe it? OMG, like, I was completely alone, well, almost, except for Little O. Let's go!" I exclaimed.

"Honey, come on dear, a monkey?" Dad scoffed at me. "That's not safe. I know this experience frightened you, but your imagination got carried away."

"But it's the truth, not my imagination. And one more time, he's an orangutan. You should know that." I scowled at Dad. "Come on, please. You'll see. He's my friend and he helped me. Now it's our turn to help him. It's only fair."

"What do you say Gita? Shall we walk to the market?" Dad asked of our new house helper.

Gita smiled at me with a twinkle in her eyes and I

knew she understood. "Yes, Mr. John, we happy to walk to market." She looked over at Zaqi. "Ya?"

Zaqi's eyes lit up as he nodded.

On the way to the market we shuffled through the gate past the guard who smiled at us. Crossing the street felt like a dangerous game of dodge ball—skirting between scooters, bikes, becaks, and motorcycles. Once we got to the market, I grabbed Dad's hand and held it tight. Luckily Dad remembered exactly where he had found me.

"He's over there." Slowly I moved my head in the direction of Little O, but the grownups were blind to him. Zaqi spotted the baby orangutan immediately. His eyes burst open, staring at me like I'd stepped off a rocket ship. We all walked closer until I raised my hand like a traffic cop. "Now stop. Stay here Dad. Promise? Just watch."

"But Jaylynn, that's not smart," he protested.

That's when I shot him an irritated look, "Please, Dad."

Slowly I walked toward Little O. When I turned around, I caught Zaqi leaning out of his shoes itching to come with me.

"Want to meet him? If you can be quiet, come with."

"Meet baby orangutan? I see in books. Ya." Turning to Gita, he asked, "*Oke ibu?*"

Gita smiled and nodded. "*Ya.*"

Walking very slowly, we approached Little O and sat down quietly. Little O stared into Zaqi's eyes for a long time.

"He sucks your breath away, right? Little O, this is Zaqi. Zaqi, this is Little O." But neither listened to me as they gawked at each other like a staring contest had begun. Finally, Zaqi gulped in a breath.

"Little O, you wonderful. But why here? Missy Jaylynn wish he talk. This place rotten for baby orangutan. No safe. Where food? Water? Where *Ibu?*"

Then Little O climbed into my lap wrapping his arms around my shoulders.

"Missy Jaylynn, he love you."

"So, like cut the Missy thing. Just call me Jaylynn."

"*Ya*... Jaylynn."

Out of the corner of my eye, Dad rocked restlessly on his heels but when he started to walk towards us, Gita reached out her arm, smiling and stopping him. Maybe she was a magician who could stop Dad. Also, it seemed like I could trust Zaqi.

"So, here's the deal. After meeting Little O, I promised him I'd get him back to the rainforest. Not clear what happened to his mom but he's hungry and miserable. And like you said, it's not safe here. Truthfully, you'll be shocked when you hear the whole story."

Zaqi exhaled scratching his head. "How you save?"

"I haven't a clue," I shrugged.

"I help?"

Zaqi could be a big help. He knew the language, the city, and liked Little O, and Little O wasn't frightened of him. Twirling my hair around my fingers, I said, "Yes, of course, you can help."

"Where rainforest?"

"His rainforest must be close. We'll figure it out," I said softly, turning to Little O.

Little O looked up at me. Yellow filled my head, warming me from the inside out. After that, I sent buckets of yellow back and grinned into Little O's sweet black eyes, rubbing his back, happy to get the hang of this color talking thing. Truthfully, I'm surprised I didn't tell Zaqi about it except he'd think I was nuts.

"Ya, sit with orangutan. I not believe." Zaqi shook his head, his smile broadening across his face.

"I love you, Little O. I promise we'll come back."

When Dad and Gita walked up, Little O jumped out of my lap, sprinting away as fast as he could and as far away as that big heavy chain let him. He huddled next to the wall. "Poppoppoppoppoppop" Afraid. A blast of red showered me.

"He's alarmed to the max. Look, he's shaking. And his lips smack together making a that sound. He's not afraid of me or Zaqi."

"It looks like grownups scare him," Dad told me. "Maybe we're too big or maybe a grownup hurt him. Hard to tell."

I whispered to Zaqi "Should we tell them our plan?"

"I not know" he responded.

"You two whispering secrets already?" Dad asked.

"We want to help him return to the rainforest because we both know he's not safe here. Dad, he helped me when I couldn't find you which is why I can't leave him here now. He's in danger."

"Jaylynn, it's an orangutan for goodness sake. He's wild. He's not a pet. How could you help him?"

"But we can't leave him here! He must get back to the rainforest, that's his home. He's all alone," I muttered, glancing over at Little O.

My lips started to quiver, a sure sign tears were coming which would be embarrassing times ten. After everything we'd been through, how could I abandon him? And let Maniac Man beat him again? When tears started to drop, I chewed on my lower lip hoping to stop the flood. Red coursed through my body as Little O talked to me in the only way he knew how.

"*Ya Ibu*," Zaqi said to Gita joining in their plea.

"Please understand. I can't leave him," I protested.

Dad shrugged, pursing his lips and shaking his head no. He swiped at his nose placing his hand on his chin. "I said no."

"But he's not safe here. You'd understand if you heard the whole story," I retorted.

Dad's face welded into a look of total frustration as his eyebrows moved together. Deep furrows formed on his forehead. "No. Jaylynn. Plain and simple, I said no."

Zaqi opened his mouth as if ready to say something, but Gita gently laid her hand on his shoulder, silencing him.

"Dad, I told him you'd help." Truthfully after losing me, I couldn't believe that he was refusing to help Little O.

"Sorry kids, but now is not the time for saving orangutans," he growled.

There always comes a point when arguing with Dad that his face turned hard as a rock. Mt. Rushmore hard. That's when you give in and obey his rules, no room for discussion. That time was now.

In an instant, my heart tore in two with red splashing everywhere. "But what can I do?" I whispered to Zaqi, "Any idea how to get them to help us?"

"No, not know. *Ibu* and Mr. John no help. I no forget him," he replied.

"Me neither. He needs our help." After that, I walked over to Little O and looked him in the eyes. "The grownups refuse to help us. But no worries. We'll be back and you're heading back to your mother and the rainforest. I promise," I said slowly.

Zaqi tiptoed over to say good bye. "I help Little O. *Salamat tinggal.*"

Alarmed by his silence and sad, mournful eyes, I touched his soft coat. Again, I sent the strongest bunch of yellow imaginable but received nothing in return. Little O had stopped talking. "Please Little O, believe me. Please don't be mad at me. You can count on me. You helped me and now I'll help you get back to your rainforest. I will." But a stab of grey hit me like a heavy woolen blanket carpeting my heart.

"Time to go now, Jaylynn. We've had a long day."

I hated leaving Little O all alone, but Zaqi and I joined our parents and as we walked away, I turned my head toward Little O, still sending yellow till I couldn't see him anymore.

Zaqi's eyes told me he understood as he whispered to me, "*Terima kasi.*"

My head tilted, not understanding.

"Mean 'thank you' in Bahasa Indonesia."

The words sounded nice and I grinned at Zaqi. "We'll rescue Little O, right?"

"*Ya*, we help baby orangutan. Rainforest, *ya.*"

"Free Little O. Even if the grownups won't help."

CHAPTER 7

DAY TWO CONTINUES

Zaqi, Dad, Gita, and I wound through the market, far away from Little O. I sent him all the yellow I could until a whiff of something awful messed with my concentration.

"Hey, what's that horrible stink? It's worse than wet skunk."

As Dad sniffed the air, his face pinched into wrinkles like a raisin. "Phew, it's ghastly! What can that be?"

Excited about something, Zaqi bounced around, his hair flopping up and down. "Here," he said pointing at a stack of weird looking greenish yellow balls with brown thick thorny things all over. "*Ibu, kami membeli durian, ya?*" Zaqi bubbled over with excitement.

He had to be joking. *Boys! I never knew for sure.* After picking it up, I spun it around. "It looks like an armored avocado ready for a fight! What's it for?"

Gita, who had been very quiet, smiled at Dad with her dark, gentle eyes. "Mr. John, Missy Jaylynn, eat durian ya? Hmm…" She stopped, maybe looking for words. "Durian best fruit in Medan. …hmm… Zaqi, you tell durian."

Zaqi immediately lowered his head, obviously not ready for more talking. Sometimes grownups missed it entirely, especially Dad. They expected their kids to talk when they didn't want to and then got frustrated when they wouldn't perform. But Gita didn't push with commands, in her gentle way she patiently gave him time.

Impatient as always, Dad pushed his glasses back up his nose. "So, what about durian?"

Gita smiled but her eyes held a secret like a cat that ate the family goldfish. I wondered what she had up her sleeve. "Buy durian, king of fruits. *Ya?*" she said. Gita borrowed a knife from the shop keeper and handed it to Zaqi.

"*Terima kasih, Ibu*" he responded.

"It sort of looks like a squeaky porcupine dog toy but I'm in. How about you, Dad?"

"Well, we moved to Sumatra to learn about life here. I'm in."

Zaqi's smile grew enormous as if he'd grabbed a double scoop chocolate chip ice cream waffle cone. Was this fruit better than my favorite candy? Wishing I knew him better, I observed a mischievous glint in his eyes as he paused, holding the knife above the durian. Then, with one quick stroke the fruit split in half, releasing the foulest stench I ever smelled. Filling my nose like paint, it reeked way worse than wet skunk. To get the disgusting odor out, I batted at my nose, but it was stuck inside. "That's awful. Like rotten, reeking, sweaty socks left under a damp towel for a week."

Even though I held my breath for as long as I could, then shielded my nose with my hand and whirled around, that stink stayed in the air. My fingers clamped together hard on my nose. "Dad, save us!"

Holding his nose, wrinkling up his eyes and waving the

air around with his other hand, he said, "You pranked us. I wasn't expecting that stink! You really eat that?"

Judging by the beam on both of their faces, the answer was yes. Not even holding his nose, Zaqi used his fingers to scoop the gooey fruit that looked like custard out of the shell. He slurped it into his mouth licking each finger, like a chocolate chip cookie warm out of the oven, beyond delicious, heavenly.

"How can you get past the smell? It makes me want to throw up." Still holding my nose, I watched Zaqi, engrossed in the joy of eating every ounce.

"Gita," Dad said, "I've never smelled anything that pungent that was actually good to eat."

Mental note to self, avoid all things pungent!

"Here, eat, ya?" Gita held out the fruit to me and Dad. We looked at each other and then at the fruit. Together we shook our heads, "Not this time, no thank you."

On the way home, straggling behind Dad and Gita, Zaqi and I talked about every little detail that we could remember about our very cool, new friend—the baby orangutan. Hard to imagine that in a blink of an eye since moving to Sumatra, my full concentration swung from me missing everything, to saving a baby orangutan.

"I like eyes because same color as me and I like face. I want cuddle him like you do," Zaqi said.

"Yes, he's very sweet to cuddle but still a wild animal, right? How old do you think he is?" Then I whispered "I want to go back there. Maybe we could feed him. You too? Even if Dad says no, I'd go. How about you?"

Kicking up dirt as he walked, Zaqi made a face like he'd

eaten something horrible. "What? You go Dad say no?"

Shrugging my shoulders and rolling my eyes, I said, "Yeah. If we're sneaky, Dad won't find out. How about you if your mom said no?"

"I want see him again. If *Ibu* say no, no lie to her. Maybe they say yes. *Ya?*"

Based on the expression of pure worry on Zaqi's face, sneaking to the market wasn't a yes. Who knew when that crazy Maniac Man would beat Little O again? Little O's life was on the line. If I could find my way to the market by myself, it was a risk I'd take.

CHAPTER 8

NIGHT TWO

At the end of another long day, Dad came in to say good night and I could see the dark cloud that Grandma called 'The Great Sadness' hovering over his head. Grandma had told me that he missed Mom, and that I hadn't done anything wrong. She said they'd figure it out and not to worry about them, but it was hard. My shoulders tensed when I saw him, but he surprised me and smiled.

"Things are going great here on our second day. Gita makes delicious food and you and Zaqi are friends. So, what's on your mind?"

"Worried about Little O all alone. Why is he chained up? It's not safe."

"Anything else you want to talk about?"

"DAD LISTEN TO ME! I'M SO NOT KIDDING!" I yelled. "TRUTHFULLY, I TOLD YOU A REALLY IMPORTANT THING. I FOUND ONE GOOD REASON TO LIVE IN SUMATRA. THE ONLY THING. LITTLE O. HE MISSES HIS MOM AND SHE'S FAR AWAY. HE'S HUNGRY AND THIRSTY. SCARED AND ALONE. AND I'M GOING TO SAVE HIM."

Dad deposited his hands on my shoulders. "Honey, it'll all work out. You'll see. You're jet lagged now. We'll talk about it tomorrow."

With a snarl on my face, I glared up at Dad, wishing he understood me but knowing that wasn't going to happen anytime soon. He had plugs in his ears, not listening, not understanding, not even a smidgeon. "Right, it'll all be fine."

"Good night, honey. Get some rest. I love you, baby girl."

After that, he left the room. Baby girl? What a joke! Exasperated, my jaw stiffened. Apparently kids my age don't save orangutans. He must think I'm crazy to even try, right? Well, I'd been certain Dad would be on my side. How wrong could I have been? But Dad or no Dad, my baby orangutan rescue started now.

Unable to fall asleep, I flipped from side to side, punching my pillow with clenched fists. UMPFHF! BAM! WOMP! BAM! BAM! BAM!

Jerking up in bed, I whacked my forehead. Little O was alone tonight. No mom, and on the end of that heavy chain, with no safety from Maniac Man's beatings. If I couldn't find a way to get him back to the rainforest, he'd never be free again.

My mission. My most important thing. And what was he doing now? Then it hit me. All I had to do was sneak out of the house for the first time in my entire life. If I made it all the way to the market, we'd cuddle till morning. We'd trade yellow signals and I'd protect him. Or if I could get him off that chain, he'd come home. Dad would have to let me keep him then.

As quietly as possible, I threw on some clothes and my flip flops and tiptoed down the stairs without one creak. Holding my hand on the door knob, aware that this might be a terrible idea, I breathed so deeply that a stone would never find the bottom. If caught, Dad would be mega-mad and ground me till I turned twenty-one. If something happened to me out there all alone, well, no use worrying. No time to chicken out now.

Unlatching the lock, inching the door open, stopping as soon as it creaked, holding my breath, listening, and as stealth as a fox, I slipped away from safety into the dark. Sprinting across the lawn gave me a tiny drop of confidence, but that quickly disappeared when I spotted the guard at the gate. A gun strapped to his waist brought visions of me leaping in the air, ducking down low and jagged sidestepping to dodge bullets. Lowering to the ground and pressing myself flat against the grass, keeping him under surveillance for what seemed like forever. A blue light lit up his face. His phone. Would he be too distracted to see me? The image of Little O, alone and afraid, pushed me forward. Time to be brave.

I sucked in a giant inhale, held my breath and slinked under the parking barrier. Just inches from the guard, feeling with my hands, my fingers grabbing wet weeds to pull me along. Keeping my head down, mysterious things swiped across my face. Every slimy thing felt like a snake and I imagined every crawly thing on my arms was a poisonous spider as I slithered around on night patrol. I crept on my belly until I was far from enough from the guard station.

Then, I stood up. *Phew!* Now, if I could only remember how to get to the market. A flashlight would have been handy. Everything looked different in the dark. Hunched over like a secret agent, I tiptoed along scanning for trouble. Then, I froze solid as an iceberg.

A dog, a big black dog, stood still as a statue on the sidewalk ahead of me. His head lowered and the fur on his back bristled straight up like a wolf. The only sound was a low, threatening growl, so low that even though I barely heard it, the hair on the back of my neck stood up. Even from a distance, his eyes glowed yellow. He didn't move a muscle. He was stalking prey—ready for the kill. Immediately, five more dogs joined him, all as still as death, and all with their eyes pinned to me. A pack of wild dogs looking straight at me. Together a growl rumbled through the dark night.

My entire body trembled. Like a frightened deer, unable to move, my fists clenched tight, my nails dug into my palms. Could I outrun a mad dog? Six mad dogs? Was I fast enough? Could I climb a tree like they tell you do when a bear chases you?

As they began to creep towards me like lions hunting their quarry, they all moved as one. If my soccer coach had told the truth about my crazy fast speed, running rather than tree climbing seemed like the right choice. If not, well, I didn't want to think about that. I glanced behind me to check the distance back to the gate. Would I be chewed up in big bites? Ripped to shreds? Unrecognizable?

GO! I spun around fast and in that split second, the dogs took off after me. Their bark said kill. When I glanced over my shoulder, the lead dog was gaining on me, closing the gap, ready to launch. Soon I felt his breath on my ankles, then his razor-sharp teeth grazed my skin and grabbed onto my pant leg. I yanked as hard as I could, away from his jaw as the fabric ripped. I started sprinting with every ounce of speed I could muster. The guard looked surprised as I flew past him, surprisingly not worried about his gun. I kept running hard.

He yelled something in Bahasa. Then, a dog yelped in pain and another squealed.

No way was I stopping. When the guard yelled again, it was as if rockets attached to my feet and I sped away. *Please don't shoot me!* Just like that, I was back at our house, slamming into our front door and opening it as fast as I could. I stood stunned on the other side, panting loudly. By some miracle, I was safe with only a torn pant leg. Heart racing. Body shaking. *Quiet! Don't wake Dad. Your life will be over.* What if the guard followed me? And knocked on the door? What was I thinking? Killed by dogs? Shot by the guard? Or caught by Dad? My breath came in gasps, but I had to be quiet.

Still panting, I tiptoed upstairs quiet as a ghost. Safe in my room, I flopped onto my bed and hid under the covers without even a thought about my torn clothes. Scary images of dogs and their razor-sharp teeth flooded my head. Lying in bed under my covers, my pillow covering my head, my eyes closed and dragged me into a deep sleep.

CHAPTER 9

DAY THREE

The next morning when I awoke, my head felt as if bats were zooming around inside of it. Remembering my stupid escapade from last night, I whacked my head. Lucky, I got out with just my pants shredded and not my leg. Stupid move! How was I going to save Little O if I couldn't make it to the market?

Stretching my arms up overhead like a cat, then scratching my belly, the screaming hunger pangs from my stomach let me know I needed breakfast. After that, stumbling over the unpacked boxes, I followed my nose towards unfamiliar aromas.

"Good morning. Come, sit down, Jaylynn. You look a little frazzled. Sleep okay?" Dad asked. "Gita has a good breakfast ready. Rice with vegetables. Fried egg on top and some spicy hot sambal!"

Strange aromas especially in the morning sent my hunger packing. My fake smile hid my disappointment about rice for breakfast. Give me a bowl of Cheerios with some toast and jam! "I'm not that hungry this morning," I replied. Before anyone noticed that I was lying through my teeth, I said, "Maybe I'll drink a glass of milk instead?"

"Now Jaylynn, it's not polite to turn down food," Dad growled like a German Shepherd. "Sit now and eat your breakfast," he commanded.

Before voicing my grumble, I rolled my eyes and bit my lower lip. What messed him up this morning? "Whatever." I squinted a quick look at Dad out of the corner of my eye and plopped in my chair. A sigh escaped. When I grow up and raise my own kids, there will be no ordering them around. I'll be a gentle Golden Retriever mother.

"Let me get glass of milk, Missy Jaylynn," Gita said. "Take time for life in Sumatra, *madu*. Eat *Nasi Goreng* tomorrow, *ya?*" And with that she saved me for the first of many times.

Obviously, I was being stubborn by not tasting the nasty whatever-she-called-it, maybe tomorrow because right now, I wasn't ready to eat that stuff first thing in the morning. But even after I chugged two glasses of milk, hunger gnawed at my stomach.

"Friday, we're off to the mall to shop for school supplies, uniforms for school and some new clothes." Dad smiled at me as if he was confident that I loved nothing more than a trip to the mall, as if he was positive that shopping meant a great day for me, but I couldn't stand it. At home, I hated shopping trips, but I was going to need a new pair of pants. Finally, Dad noticed my silence.

"Jaylynn, you feeling sick? You've hardly eaten a thing. I thought you'd be excited about going to the mall. Trouble sleeping? Jet lag can be a problem."

"That must be it Dad." Trying out my Class A Lie.

"Having a hard time locating my brain today. Must be that jet lag thing. Okay if I leave the table? I'm not that hungry. Maybe I'll check my email."

"That's fine."

When I went online, an email from Matt, my best friend back home, made my day. I couldn't open it fast enough.

Dear Jay,

Can't believe you're so far away. I keep looking at our globe and wow, 8,000 miles away, amazing. I pulled up some photos of Medan, and it must be crazy to live there. Looks crowded, lots of scooters. You made any friends? Life drags dull without you. Mom and Dad said hi and told me that we could Skype. Ask your Dad. Bought some Pop Tarts yesterday. Write me back as soon as you can.

Matt

Immediately, I emailed Matt about the orangutan and sneaking out. He was going to be shocked that I became a juvenile delinquent in three days. Realizing that I knew nothing about orangutans, I googled 'orangutans in Indonesia.'

Zaqi walked in and asked, "What you read?"

"Looking up orangutans. Here sit down and we can read together."

"I sorry. I not read fast English."

"Your English is like way better than my zero Bahasa. Let's see if the computer will translate to Bahasa Indonesia."

With windows opened side by side in English and Bahasa, we buried our noses in the information.

"They smart. Read here," Zaqi said.

"They use leaves as umbrellas and to drink water, too. They sleep in nests that they build high up in trees. Hey, Little O doesn't have a nest," I said.

"No. Only dirt. Poor O." Zaqi paused. "What eat?"

"Right here it says that they eat mostly shoots and roots but bugs and little animals, too. No way, look, their treat matches yours—durian!" I squealed. "Hey, let's go to the market and buy him a durian."

"*Ya?*"

"Little O's rescue starts now," I said. "Let's break it down. How do we get him?"

"He for sale? Maybe we buy?"

My fingers twirled around a strand of hair, while I thought of solutions. "There's some money in my savings account in Seattle but Dad won't let that happen. Or we steal him? Right? How hard could that be? What if we slip him out of his collar?"

Zaqi gawked at me like I'd told him we planned to rob a bank. "Steal? Not good. Bad thing. Take to jail! We be criminals. Never get out. Big fine. Steal not good. I no do to *Ibu*." Zaqi's face scrunched up like he'd swallowed sour milk. "They catch us. Against law. They arrest."

"They'd send kids to jail? Not give us a second chance?" Guess he was right about jail. That would be a problem but still, I imagined the newscast. Two young people hauled off to jail today, in handcuffs, for stealing an orphaned baby orangutan. They said they wanted to bring him back to the rainforest. And then our photos flash on the screen.

"Ibu be sad. No do. No steal." With that he crossed his arms, frowning at me.

"Yeah, yeah, you're right. Just joking. But truthfully, I don't know how to get enough money to buy him. Maybe I can steal some money from my dad's wallet?"

Zaqi's mouth dropped open again.

"Just joking Zaqi. I'd never do that."

"You steal money from Dad. I not help. No steal. Ibu tell me always way when heart say yes. Save Little O," Zaqi smiled at me, his eyes twinkling.

Definitely good to believe there was always a way, but we needed a plan. Not stealing since I needed Zaqi's help. Or I just wouldn't tell him. Mom said acting like a grownup meant following all the rules but that wasn't going to work here.

"I not know how. But *Ibu* say always solution. Look up on computer now. Save Little O," Zaqi smiled at me, his eyes twinkling.

"Right." I raised my eyebrows and gave him my sneaky spy nod. We were going to rescue Little O. Somehow. I knew it.

Zaqi googled rainforests. "Mount Leuser, Kerinci Seblat and Bukit Barisan National Parks." His look said it all.

"Three? That's two too many. How can we figure out which one? My mom would call this situation a prickly dingle."

We both went quiet.

"Okay let's say we figure out, somehow, which one has his mother. How do we get him there?" I searched my head for any ideas. "We need transportation. Bus? Train? Car? Wish I could drive."

"I have idea. Cousin has scooter and he let us use… maybe."

"A scooter? How old is your cousin? You know how to drive?"

"Not know but learn. Bima thirteen."

"Say what? He can drive and he's only 13 and you can drive and you're 11? And he has a scooter? So, if he lets us, we drive to the rainforest? I hold on to you and Little O holds on to me? That's a crazy image. Will it work, you think?"

When I pictured the three of us on a scooter, two kids and a baby orangutan, holding on tight, the giggling started until my eyes watered. Trying my hardest to laugh quietly, only made me laugh more, and when Zaqi joined in, our laughter went wild. "My face hurts from laughing." I tried to regain control. "Every time I picture the three of us on a scooter holding on to each other, I crack up. Wonder if Little O ever rode on a scooter? The uproar will freak him out."

"Here, whole family on scooter," Zaqi explained. "Mom, Dad, and kids, same scooter."

"You ever seen two kids and a baby orangutan? Should we dress him up like a baby?" Imagining a cartoon with me holding a hairy baby with a little blue hat and outfit, little gasps of giggles kept sneaking out until I lost myself to laughter again. "Sorry, so let's say that your cousin says yes. Priority number one is to keep Little O safe, you know."

"That problem. I never drive. But I learn. How hard it be?" Zaqi knitted his dark eyebrows together as if trying to convince himself.

"You talk to your cousin and see if he'll help us. He can keep a secret from your mother, right?"

"We go cousin house tonight. If he say yes, then we ride. Then we see if we can buy Little O, *ya?*"

"You get a scooter and learn to drive it and then we'll deal with the next thing—WHERE." I said. "I gotta talk to Matt about all of this."

"Dad, Dad," I yelled. Can I Skype Matt now? Think he'll be up? I can't wait to see what he says about Little O."

"Jaylynn, you're still talking about that orangutan?"

"Of course, I'm talking about him. Help me Skype."

That day two things occupied my mind: 'How to make Money Quickly in Medan, Sumatra' and 'How to Steal Little O.' Time to Skype Matt and get some ideas.

I filled him in... "Now you know everything." Hearing his voice calmed most of the jitters that had been bouncing around my head. "Zaqi handles our escape vehicle and I come up with the cash."

"Sounds like a crime. Your life is amazing. Seattle is so boring."

"Figure you could help us with our plan."

"Help? You need my help? Freakin' awesome! An orangutan? A scooter? Find the rainforest and then like somehow Little O's mother? OMG tell me what you need me to do. He sits in your lap? Dude, I'm so jealous."

"Yeah, I love him so much and we've got to get him out of there, right? But I don't have the money to buy him."

"Who lives in Medan that you could ask for help? Ask kids at school. It starts soon, right?"

After a dramatic eye roll, I reminded him that school started on Monday and I knew no one. "I'm not positive they're ready for this question: 'Hi, I want to buy a baby orangutan for sale in the market and set it free in the rainforest. Yeah and don't tell anyone. It's a huge secret and maybe illegal.' How's that sound to you?" A strand of hair twirled around my finger.

"Right. So, when will you know if you can buy him and for how much?" Matt asked.

Next thing I knew, my head hit the desk as my fists pounded it.

"No time for pounding. We'll find a way." Matt placed his hand on his chin, rubbing back and forth looking like some old professor.

Twirling a strand of hair around my finger, my confidence wobbled around as much as my first time on roller blades…heading for a crash. Before moving here, my biggest life moment had been one soccer goal, the only one that I scored last year because the whole team backed me up. Who would be on my team in Indonesia? Only Zaqi. Matt called this the best adventure ever, but it felt like life or death for Little O, way more than an adventure and it all depended on me.

"Got it," he said. "Here's our plan. From the U.S., I hold a fundraiser here with all our friends but keep it on the down low. Everyone donates maybe $5. Maybe a week ago, I saw an ad on TV that you can wire money across the world. So, we find out if 11-year-old kids can wire money. I'll get on that right away."

"Nice!" I nodded back, happy to get his help.

"Do you think any of the kids in your school can keep a secret and help The Great Orangutan Rescue to save Little O's life?"

"Maybe? I'm the new kid, remember. When he's not around, I could start sneaking money out of my dad's wallet or I could look through his desk. He won't even notice."

"WHAT? Jaylynn, you can't do that! You'll get caught. Jaylynn snap out of it. What are you thinking? NO! I'll do my best to get you money. Don't start stealing from your Dad. Do you hear me?"

"Yeah, I guess. But honestly, it would be easier. Okay but I'm not promising. The point is I've got to save Little O. Remember, secrecy keeps the plan alive. No parents or somehow, it'll get back to Mom or Dad and they'll blow up like dynamite."

The plan had wheels if it stayed secret. If Dad found out, a long walk off a short plank was in store for me and if he saw me riding a scooter—house arrest. Meanwhile, stealing Little O still seemed like an easier choice, well, if it didn't involve jail or Maniac Man. Scheming and lying and plotting... my life in Indonesia was shaping up into a big bag of adventure, massively different from life in Seattle.

CHAPTER 10

NIGHT THREE

Later than night Zaqi burst into my bedroom with an uptight expression on his face, no smile, furrowed brow, and gloomy eyes—all forecasting bad news.

"I go Bima house ask him borrow scooter. All I hear giant rain of 'no, no, NO' from Bima stomp on whole idea."

"Dude. Really? What's his deal?" Disappointment wormed its way into my brain, because there was no backup plan for driving Little O to the rainforest.

"He say not safe me drive. He say not safe us drive orangutan. He say parents very angry. He say not find mother orangutan and not leave baby in rainforest. He say if wreck scooter, get hurt, *Ibu* wreck him. He big flood all reason why bad idea."

The winds of doubt smashed into my head. Saving Little O meant living in a mood swing torture chamber, a roller coaster of good and bad. With no solution in sight, I rolled a strand of hair around my finger and drew in a deep breath. "That's horrible. So, we need to find another scooter or another way. That's all there is to it."

A dark cloud covered Zaqi's face, making him look like

a forlorn puppy abandoned at birth. He continued, "I tell about Little O, how sweet baby. What life like, how sad, prisoner in jail. I tell Bima Little O Indonesian wild animal and our job protect. And then I quiet. Bima say he want see Little O. Good idea, *ya?*"

"Of course, yes, a great idea. Brilliant! We'll get to see Little O, too, and your cousin will love him. We can bring him durian. I like his name even if he said no to our dream."

"Name mean extraordinary. He work long time, save money, buy scooter. It old but he love it and proud."

"Nice. Let's see if he can meet us tomorrow. Will our parents let us go alone with him?

"*Ibu say ya.*"

"Well, then Dad will too, maybe, if we don't tell him we're riding the scooter. Can I tell you a secret?"

"*Ya.*"

I told Zaqi the full story about sneaking out, the guard station, the dog ripping my pant leg, my racing away and sneaking back into the house and into bed. Of course, I left out the crying. No way was I ready to admit to that!

"You brave. But not safe. You not go anymore. What your name mean?"

"Jaylynn? It means nothing. Honestly, I mean, I wish. Mom wanted to name me after her favorite aunt, Lynn, and Dad wanted to name me after his favorite teacher, Jay. They put it together and I'm Jaylynn."

"I give you name. I call you *Wani.*"

"*Wani?* What does it mean?"

"Daring."

Laughing at my new name, I grinned at him, shaking

my head no. "Daring? I'm a mile away from that. Not what I'd ever call myself. 'Chicken' is more like it." My new name bounced around in my head until even I had to admit I liked it. "Maybe I'll grow into it? The next time I sneak out! Maybe you'll come? What's your name mean?"

"'Zaqi' mean smart." Zaqi shook his head, rolling his eyes. "Not sneak out."

"Okay, I get it. No sneaking out. Thanks for the new name. Time for sleep!"

Rifling through the mess on my desk, I grabbed a notebook and at the top of the page wrote "LITTLE O'S GREAT RESCUE PLAN by Jaylynn O'Reilly" and below the title, I wrote:

WHO? Me and Zaqi

WHEN? Who knows

HOW? No idea

WHERE? Have to figure that out.

Then I stared blankly, looking for answers, but nothing appeared except Dad smiling at me.

"What are you working on?"

He sat beside me and I lifted my head wondering which Dad had walked into my room. Lately, Dad moved from steady St. Bernard to growling German Shepherd with no warning.

"I'm working on my new job now and making a plan."

Dad's eyes closed for a moment and I heard him suck in a deep breath. "Little O?"

"Yes. He's the best thing about Sumatra so far. Especially without Mom here. Guess she forgot about me. I miss her."

"She'd would never forget you but it's hard to explain what's going on with her. She's on a quest with her job… to feel successful in her profession. I know that's tough on you."

Without meaning to, my eyes rolled. "Yeah, you can say that again," I said. Without thinking, my sarcastic tone popped out, the one that usually aggravated him.

Luckily, he only cleared his throat. "If you're having trouble living here, talk to me. I'll listen. I can't make your problems go away but how about if we let them jump off your back and onto mine?"

"Can I Skype Mom now?"

"Sure, give her a call."

Mom sounded excited to hear from me and we talked for over an hour. When I told her all about getting lost and then finding Little O, giving her every little detail about him, except the part about color talking, she seemed pleased. And I told her about Maniac Man and the scary escape, but I left out the part about sneaking out. I watched her face trying to see inside her heart. Like with Little O, I wondered what color she'd send me.

"I can't believe everything that's happened, Jay. It frightens me to picture all of it. That Maniac Man sounds horrible, but you managed to escape him, thank goodness. I'm so proud of you, remembering the self-defense class. What did your dad say about that man?

"I haven't told him about that part, not yet anyway."

"Wish I was there to help. You have a cell phone now so call me anytime. It's so good to see and hear from you!"

"Sure Mom. Wish you could give me a hug."

"Me, too. Jaylynn. Listen, about the orangutan... It's a big project. Can you get your dad to help?"

"You kidding? He still calls it a monkey and refuses to help me... but at least he's here."

"Well, I'm with you 100% on your mission to save Little O. Make a plan, honey. Make a list of what needs to happen and then figure out who and how you'll need to get each step accomplished. Think it through."

Frustration building, I answered in a voice full of sharp tacks and nails. "You're telling me that I can solve this?" I said in a harsh voice. "I only know how to say 'thank you' in Bahasa and you figure I can pull off this rescue? It's going to be like a bank robbery. Why doesn't anyone understand? How can I get him back to his rainforest all by myself?"

"I understand that you're capable and you'll figure it out. Call anytime."

After that call, happiness and sorrow played against each other with no clear winner. Remembering my old life in Seattle, my simple life, I wondered how it turned into a complicated mess. Who turned the bucket upside down, spilling me and Dad into Indonesia and Mom into Washington, D.C. like pieces from a board game? All our fun family stuff landed somewhere in the middle of the ocean, likely sunk to the bottom by now.

And my life? They spun me around like a top with no say so. I shook my head to clear out aggravating, worthless brainwaves. Enough of parents. I had a demanding job—find Little O's rainforest and the safety of his mom. I thought about sneaking out again to see Little O, but when my head hit the pillow, sleep won an easy battle with my eyelids.

CHAPTER 11

NIGHT THREE ENDS

Stretching my arms up overhead, I wrapped them around a tall tree covered in big, ropelike vines in the dense, dark jungle. My legs bent around the trunk as my feet pushed into the cool, ridged bark. Barefoot, my toes gripped the tree bark like monkey feet, making me climb with ease. Birds screeched all around me in a cacophony as up I rose higher and higher.

Bugs swarmed around my face getting caught in my eyelashes, humming in my ears, driving me crazy. When one big bug flew straight up my nose, I huffed harder and harder trying to blow it out of my nose, but it crawled inside and totally grossed me out. Afraid of a bug stuck up my nose, I used my little finger to pick it out and then put it in my mouth to eat. Crunchy!

My balance faltered and though I tried to grip the tree with my fingers and toes, I started falling backwards, head over heels, tumbling downward, faster and faster. The limb I grabbed on to, slipped through my fingers. I spun over and over, faster and faster. As I crashed through leaves and branches and plummeted to earth, I knew that soon I'd crash into the ground, breaking all my bones. Then, unexpectedly, out of nowhere, a hand reached out and grabbed me, firmly! *Oomph*! I dangled in mid-air, completely stopped, my feet twisted around. After taking a slow, deep breath, I took a quick look down. Still a long way to the ground—my heart beat wildly. *Phew. What happened?* Slowly, I raised my eyes to see who or what grabbed me and the lovely face of a beautiful orangutan, full of kindness and grace, gazed straight into my eyes. From somewhere, I sensed yellow filling my heart like talking to Little O and sent yellow back. The big orangutan pulled me up to safety to sit next to her on a thick branch.

"Ah, young orangutan, still learning to live in the rainforest I see. Let me help you learn to build a nest to sleep in tonight." she said in a quiet low voice. "We will climb back up, pick a strong spot and then start building with leaves and branches. Come."

"Are you my mother?"

"No. Call me Auntie. Here, these leaves are good to eat. Pull the bark off in this spot and look for bugs to eat. Keep building your nest. You will sleep there tonight."

I gathered leaves and branches building a nest high about the ground surrounded by green, the dampness of the rainforest, birds screeching while plucking insects and tasting their crunchy, juicy bodies.

"I know a baby orangutan. He lives in the market. Do you know him?" I said.

"Yes. I know this baby. You must bring him to the rainforest."

"But how?" I whispered in complete disbelief. "How

can I get him here? Tell me where I am? Where is his mother?"

"Go to sleep and rest. You'll be the champion for the baby. You'll bring him back to the rainforest."

Sleep overwhelmed me. My eyes barely stayed open as the nest swayed gently in the breeze and the birds sang a lullaby. Peaceful and safe, I drifted into slumber but then remembered—I didn't know where I was.

"But wait, wait, I need the name of this rainforest! How can I save him without the name? Please tell me before I go to sleep. I can't stay awake… Please... please tell me."

Just then we heard men down on the rainforest ground. Through the dense foliage, I heard their voices shouting in Bahasa.

"Quick. Hide from those men. Get in your nest. They want to steal you. Sleep. Stay safe."

"But tell me where I am? How do I find his mother?"

The orangutan slipped quietly away lost behind the dense green foliage. But right before I fell asleep, I heard her whisper, "You are in Gunung Leuser."

My eyes slipped shut but over and over I said to myself: "Gunung Leuser, Gunung Leuser, Gunung Leuser."

A gunshot blast woke me from this vivid dream. Who shot that gun? What happened? Where did Auntie go? She said I was an orangutan? I must get back to her.

I closed my eyes willing myself to go back to sleep, knowing I needed way more information, like where to find the rainforest? Everything seemed real and not a dream. Wait, she told me the rainforest's name and I must remember it to get Little O back there. Gu… or Gun...

Gut... or Gur? Gunung Leuser. I remembered it! Anxious for morning to come, I wanted to tell Dad all about my dream, certain that after he heard about the rainforest and the orangutan, he'd finally change his mind and help me rescue Little O.

CHAPTER 12

DAY FOUR

Waking up, I scratched my head, rubbed my eyes, patted my belly, and wiggled my feet—all while yawning. And then I remembered that last night in a dream, I had lived in a rainforest with an orangutan. The freshness of the damp rainforest and the orangutan's voice, warm and comforting, stayed with me. Wait, she had told me the rainforest's name and I must remember it to get Little O back there. "Gu… or Gun…Gut… or Gur?"

Rolling my eyes up to the ceiling, I strained my brain trying to remember but with no luck. Without bothering to get dressed or brush my hair or teeth, I staggered downstairs in my PJs.

"Good morning, Jaylynn!" Dad moved his tie around his neck tightening it up a bit. "I'm off to the office this morning. Still in your jammies, I see. Looks like you had another rough sleep last night."

"How did you guess? I dreamt about the rainforest, climbing high up a tree like an orangutan. I slipped and started falling fast until an orangutan, my auntie, grabbed my hand and saved me."

"You dream orangutan auntie? She never visit me in dreams. What happen?" asked Zaqi, excitedly.

I told them every detail that I could remember, and then explained the cool part. "She said the name of her rainforest…Gun-something and maybe the second word sounded like Laser or Loser. I can't believe I forgot."

"Honey, it's a dream," Dad said to reassure me.

Disappointed in Dad, who never backed me up when I needed his support, I shook my head, looking at the floor. "She told me the name."

"I bet your imagination made up a word after hearing Bahasa everywhere we go."

I sighed. Like he never listened to me. What was up with that?

"No time for dreams, sweetheart. Now eat your breakfast."

Something snapped, and I had to fight back. "No! Listen to me," I protested. "You treat me like a little kid."

Dad sat up very straight with a stern expression across his face. I knew that look and readied for trouble. "Young lady watch your mouth! What's wrong with you this morning?"

Figuring if I'm a little bit in, I might as well go all the way. I stabbed my angry finger on the table glaring at him. "WHAT SHAKES? YOU CUT ME NO SLACK WITHOUT EVEN KNOWING WHAT I'M GOING THROUGH HERE! LISTEN TO ME!" I snapped. "I know it's a real location. I need to figure it out."

"Change your tone, young lady, or go back to your room, NOW!" His face taut with anger after my outburst,

72

Dad sat in his chair with his arms crossed.

I never had fights with Dad in Seattle, maybe because of Mom. Here, that was all we did. Why didn't he get it and why wouldn't he help me? Ignoring him, I tried to remember the rainforest name. "Gun, maybe gum..."

"Keep trying," Zaqi said.

Dad studied Zaqi and then scrutinized me, but I ignored him.

"Gunlee. An 'L' in there somewhere. Gunser?"

Zaqi started combining letters, too, "Gunber? Gubber? Gunir?"

Between us, we said it a million different ways, driving Dad nuts, but then Gita interrupted us.

"*Ya*, I know this Gunung Leuser. *Ya*, Missy Jaylynn?"

"Yes. Yes. That's it!" I exclaimed, jumping out of my chair and waving my arms in the air. "It's real? We can go there?"

"Gita, that word in her dream that the orangutan told her marks a real locale?" Dad asked. "How can that be? A forest exists named Gunung Leuser?" Dad pronounced it very slowly and carefully. "But there can't be orangutans there. Right? Could her dream be real?"

"I know forest," Gita said. "Orangutan live there." Gita wrote it on paper, so we'd get the spelling right. "You look to computer. *Ya?*"

Zaqi flew out of his chair, tipping it over, and then bowed his head, his palms joining together at his heart. "Sorry, Mr. John."

Dad shook his head, waving us both off, and as we ran out of the room, I heard him sigh.

I smiled at Zaqi as we bounded up the stairs to the computer. "What the heck? Will we find orangutans there? My dream was real? Is that a little creepy?"

After a few minutes on the internet, we found it sending us whooping, hollering and dancing around. There it was, Gunung Leuser rainforest.

"It's real? Listen to this. Orangutans live there. Wild ones and even rehabilitated ones released to freedom after a life of captivity as pets. That means that now we know where Little O came from, his rainforest, and his real home. We can take him back there to live with his mom. I feel like jumping up and down. No more living in the dirt, tied to a chain, in the noisy market. So, my dream was true. I'll be the champion for the baby! We got the WHERE! Now we just need the HOW and the WHEN."

"It's the spot!" we shouted together as we ran back into the dining room, out of breath.

From the way he held his head and the frustration in his eyes, Dad seemed dangerously close to firing up the Big Kibosh, stopping my mission, but perhaps underneath his stern look there was a wee bit of excitement.

"Don't get carried away, you two. Slow down and tell us what you read."

I told him everything. "That means that now we know where Little O came from, his rainforest, his real home. We can take him back there to live with his mom. Don't you love this good news? Please, can we go see him again?" I begged.

"Slow up, honey. I admit your dream is very strange but we're going to need more research. Have you ever been to this forest, Gita?"

"No, Mr. John, long trip by car or bus. Too much money for trip. Years back, river flood there. From illegal logging. Kill people in town and wash away homes. Build again and now tourist go see orangutans," she replied.

"What a great adventure to go there. Can we?" Gazing at Dad across the table, I pleaded for a yes, making my eyes as sorrowful as possible. "Can we go? Please?"

"You kids, I'm proud of you. You really steamrolled through this with persistence and intensity. So, let's go over what you know. You think Little O came from that rainforest?"

"Yes. What else can my dream mean?" We shook our heads in total agreement. "His mom must be alive, in that rainforest, waiting for Little O. And can we please we go see her?"

"And if she does live there, how would you find her in a rainforest? Keep thinking about the logistics here before flying off the handle" Dad suggested.

I calmed myself down. If we were going to rescue Little O, I needed his help. "Okay, Dad. We'll plan, like Mom always says, and then let the rescue begin!

"I need to go to work today. You okay staying with these two?" Dad cast a gentle glance at Gita, who nodded and smiled back at us.

"Hope your first day at the office goes well. I love you, Dad."

Hearing 'I love you' stopped him dead in his tracks. He swirled around, marched back two giant steps and wrapped me up in a bear hug. I sniffed his Dad smell.

"I love you too, honey. Glad to see you happy here, even if it means orangutans take over every minute of our lives. Enjoy today with Gita. Be a good girl."

Once he left for work, we raced to the kitchen. "We want to help you with the breakfast dishes. We'll dry. I can't believe it. What a day! Let's hurry and get the dishes washed."

"*Ibu*, Bima want meet Little O. We go today, *ya?*" Zaqi asked.

"Ya, you go. Good. You make sure Jaylynn safe. Not lost." Gita put her arm around me and smiled.

"Oh good! I can meet Bima and go see Little O!" I grinned a very wide grin.

CHAPTER 13

DAY FOUR
CONTINUES

Zaqi and I headed outside and saw a lean, gangly-built boy with thick dark hair and a seemingly confident attitude. He stood next to an old turquoise scooter with chipped paint on the fenders, a little worn out cushion for a seat, and a cracked rear-view mirror. He resembled Zaqi, but taller and a little darker, more wiry and much more serious. I smiled a hello.

"I'm Bima. Climb on. Let's go!" he exclaimed. The motor roared when he fired up the engine, ready for action. Zaqi spun onto his seat and then I plopped on behind him not wanting to look like a total sissy and hoping to hide my fear. I pictured Dad in full roar ready to kill me if he knew I was on a scooter.

"How about helmets?"

Zaqi shook his head. "No helmet here."

"Right. No helmets." Was it smart to ride this thing with no helmet? I pictured rolling on the pavement after a crash holding both halves of my head together.

Without warning, we burst into motion and I slid backwards almost falling completely off the seat. At every near collision, closing my eyes, I tucked my face into Zaqi's back. The tighter I gripped, the more I squished the bananas I brought for Little O. Scared out of my wits as we bounced over every bump and pothole in the road, I became certain that I'd drop Little O if I had to hold him for hours on the drive to his rainforest. We headed right to the market and of course, as soon as Bima saw Little O, his attitude changed. They locked eyes and Bima stood in silence, in reverie, until his face transformed, to that of a very young boy, a very young boy in love. His eyes grew wide and liquid. All that serious stuff tumbled away.

"I never see anything this sweet and helpless," Bima said. He sat down near Little O, his eyes pinned on him, obviously spellbound not moving a muscle. Little O blinked up at Bima, trust in his eyes, examining Bima as if somehow, he knew this boy could help him. They stayed like that, not moving. Bima started with a little grin and it worked into a big smile. His eyes crinkled, warm. "Zaqi, Jaylynn, now I see why you want save him. He very beautiful but eyes... very sad. He need help. His life here bad. Guy in the store own him?"

"We don't know."

Bima watched Little O intently while he spoke. "And you ride scooter three to four hours to rainforest. I not certain it go that far. *Sepupu*, big plan."

I stayed quiet, watching and listening. Little O watched and listened, too. Zaqi straightened his back, a look of determination on his face.

Zaqi focused his eyes on Little O. "He not stay here. We must help him get home."

"I not believe in plan. I want help, but many things go wrong, AND you must keep secret. I get in big trouble they find out it my scooter." Bima sat there and scowled for what seemed like hours. He rubbed his eyes with his hands, as if visions of trouble clouded his thoughts.

Little O looked at us, moving his eyes from Bima to Zaqi to me and then crawled into my lap. He wrapped his arms around me, enveloping me in yellow. Wish the other guys could feel the colors. Little O peeled one of the bananas and ate it fast. Bima watched me, nodding his head in approval.

Bima and Zaqi spoke in Bahasa, a grim expression on their faces, and then it got way too quiet. Little O reached out his hand to touch Bima, twisting him out of his solemn mood. Bima softened his face as he looked at the baby orangutan. "Little O, hello there. You sweet baby. Can I pet him?"

Zaqi nodded and I watched Little O make a very important friend. A friend we needed to set him free. Good work, Little O.

"You have money to buy?"

Time for a good bluff. "Uh, well, yeah, absolutely, I'll get it."

"I go in store. You want come with?" Bima said.

Shaking my head, too afraid to ever see Maniac Man again, but not willing to tell Zaqi and Bima about him. Would they help me if I told them about the beatings? And grabbing me? For now, another secret to keep. They walked into the store and I stayed with Little O cuddled on my lap.

"See Little O, we're working on this, but it's a jumbled

predicament. We're going to get you free and safe and protected. The pieces of the puzzle are coming together. And it's getting easier to understand your colors. Now green lets me picture your rainforest home high up in the trees. Wish I had money and could bring you home now. Maybe I'll come and snatch you away. Our own little heist to freedom. What do you think?" I sent him a blanket of green and in just a second, an enormous layer of green covered me. I breathed in freedom.

When Bima and Zaqi came back around the corner, they seemed pretty excited. Bima spoke first. His voice crackled. "He say ya, $200." Bima tilted his head, a look of suspicion on his face. He narrowed his eyes, tugging at his ear like a problem needed solving. "Think bad man. Not trust. Not give you Little O. I worry. How tight that collar? Maybe better steal him."

Had I heard right? "Steal Little O?"

Bima nodded. Not a speck of worry on his face like he stole orangutans away from creepy people all the time.

I moved my fingers around the collar sizing up Bima with new respect. Zaqi's cousin believed in action. "It's pretty thick and tight with a locked chain, too."

"Hmm… will he let me look at it?" Bima bent over examining the collar looking for a loose link. "No, this thing is monster. We'd never get it off." He held the chain examining each link. "Maybe right here. Maybe twist this link off."

Zaqi didn't reply to Bima's words. No way did Zaqi want us to steal him. Stealing meant going against his mother. Stealing meant jail if we were caught. Buying him avoided that catastrophe. Either way, I'd be permanently grounded if my dad found out.

"We no steal. I no help if we steal." Zaqi crossed his arms over his chest and stood strong.

No one said anything. *Should I tell them the truth about Maniac Man? Why not?*

"Not trust this man, *sepupu*." Bima and Zaqi were staring each other down. Neither one was moving or breathing.

"Let me see if I can gather up the $200 before we steal him." I said.

Bima frowned, not ready to give in. "Whole thing problem, a man I not trust, driving my scooter, bring baby orangutan to rainforest. *Ibu* not be happy." He covered his mouth with his hand and stared at Zaqi.

Zaqi hesitated and nodded his head in agreement. "Not easy. Look at Little O. How we leave him here? He Sumatran orangutan. Live on chain."

Bima looked up at the sky, then down to Little O. Zaqi must have found the magic words to change Bima's mind. "Ya, I help you two. I want baby orangutan back in rainforest, too. Zaqi, you start driving today."

Barely able to hold back my excitement, shouting a silent YES! We could do this. He agreed! We had the HOW!

As we patted Little O goodbye, each one of us whispered to him. Little O watched Bima, then Zaqi and then me, the only one who understood the big whoosh of yellow he had sent us all. Smiling back, whooshing him back a gigantic bucket of yellow.

CHAPTER 14

NIGHT FOUR

When bedtime arrived, hunger beat out sleep. After four days in Medan, rice had been my most common option. Sitting on my bed and looking at the blank walls, my stomach growled like a large animal hunting for food. I held my knees to my stomach and tried to get the ache to go away.

Drifting off, I imagined a favorite snack I ate with Mom and Dad, a giant bowl of popcorn with butter dripping off each piece. Then, an image of Matt and I, and a big juicy hamburger next to a whole pile of greasy fries drowning in a pool of ketchup. My imagination was too vivid. I swiped at my mouth to keep the saliva from dripping, rallied myself, and headed downstairs.

There had to be something in that fridge to eat, I thought. I was wearing my soccer shorts and my t-shirt from last year's soccer camp—my most prized possession. That camp had been the beginning of an entirely new life for me... well, almost. Even though smaller than the rest of the girls, when it came to dribbling the ball down the field around the defense, I got it done. Turned out that I ran faster than most and the coach said I had good feet.

I remembered the last day at camp when my coach put his arm around me and called me the most improved player. He encouraged me to stick with soccer and even called me a natural. But then Dad had told me about the move and dreams of World Cup fame ended abruptly. *El fin*. Done. Over.

Hunger brought me back to reality. Not wanting to disturb Dad or Gita, I tiptoed to the kitchen like a detective hunting for clues. "Refrigerator. Give me your good stuff now! No more rice and no more chicken. I want snacks. American snacks!"

When I opened the fridge, my eyes scanned all the shelves looking for anything: an orange, an apple, some bread, peanut butter and jelly, a cookie or piece of pie. Nothing. Absolutely nothing that I wanted to eat. I pushed things around and looked in the back.

Desperate, I opened the vegetable bin and closed it. Then the fruit bin. Like a thief in the night, I grabbed the whole bunch of bananas from the fridge and suddenly felt yellow. Little O? Is that you sending me love? My hunger was probably nothing compared to his. And he'd love even just one little banana. *Hmm...* the house was quiet. Could I sneak out and this time make it past the guard? Maybe the dogs would be gone? Definitely worth a shot.

I slipped on my flip flops, silently turned the lock, and glided out the door. First part done! Reaching the guard station, my body slipped under the fence. Out on the streets, every shadow scared me. As I wandered alone in the dark, everyone was a possible criminal and I listened for growls. Even the bushes reached out like enemies, aided by trees that loomed like super villains on the darkened street.

Finally, at the market, still full of people, I hoped no one questioned me. I mean what's a kid doing out this late? Yellow bombed me the instant I got close. Little O! Yes! How could he tell I was here? I sent back yellow. Here I come!

Stealthy as a fox, my eyes searched for Maniac Man first. Not ready to have another run in or worse—watch him beat Little O. With the bunch of bananas tucked under my arm like a football, I ran to Little O and we both made chirpy noises. Happy that my heart had led me here.

Little O hopped on my lap, grabbed the bananas, peeled each one, and gobbled them down. Starving. My little friend was as hungry as if he had never eaten a meal. Rubbing his back, I cooed to him as he gobbled down all seven bananas without once coming up once for air.

With a full belly, Little O curled up in my lap and fell asleep with one hand holding onto my hair and the other, my hand. Our breathing matched each other's and soon, I fell sleep oblivious to all the action around me. Not sure how long I slept, my head jerked up when I heard a voice, Maniac Man's voice. If Maniac Man caught me again, I might not get away. Time to move. Gently as if he was a glass doll, I lifted Little O off my lap and left him curled up sound asleep.

Walking far away from the store, my inner voice warned me. It practically shouted at me. *HIDE.*

I skyrocketed away and hid behind a stall. Like a turtle, I pulled in my head, arms, and legs, and sat listening. Then yellow turned to red and just as I turned my head to check behind me, I felt a hand grasp my arm.

Using all my strength, I jerked out of his grip. Sprinting through the market, out to the streets and past tree branches that scraped my face like claws, I didn't know how long to run, but like coach said, running was my strength.

I slowed down and looked back. Out of breath, panting, dizzy from fear, imagining him lurking in all the shadows. Out of the darkness, I heard footsteps coming fast. Maniac Man. I exploded into a run. My feet raced along the ground and I sprinted for blocks. I ran and ran so hard till I spotted the guard gate. Sprinting past the guard, in full stride, I pointed behind me, "Help me. Stop him."

Just past the swings my foot caught on something on the ground, tripping me, flying, spinning my world until I landed with a *whoomph* on the hard ground. My nose sniffed the damp grass as my eyelids opened slowly. Suddenly remembering Maniac Man and the guard, I sprung to my feet. Without looking back, I bolted all the way home, all the way upstairs, under my covers, planning to stay there forever.

As my eyes closed, I sent yellow bunches to Little O. We're coming. You'll be free. What color was free I wondered?

CHAPTER 15

DAY FIVE

In the morning, waking with a start, glancing around my room, I remembered the chase. Maniac Man knew where I lived. Did he know I might be planning to steal Little O? When Dad came in, I pulled my blanket up over my shoulder to hide my clothes.

"Honey, time for breakfast. Think Gita is frying eggs this morning."

"Yum!"

Down at the breakfast table, plotting to see Little O, I asked in my sweet voice. "Daddy, shall we stop at the market for groceries?" I cooed. My eyes twinkled as I beamed the inviting smile of a sly secret agent going in for the kill. Knowing the market meant a trip to see Little O, my sneaky smile was caught by Gita.

"Yes, Mr. John. Good to buy vegetables now." Gita winked at Zaqi and me, and I could tell she was happy to help.

Walking to the market, I dredged up the horror of my run away from Maniac Man and wondered if I should tell Zaqi. He'd made me promise not to go again. Another secret to keep to myself. They were adding up!

After getting groceries, I once again used my sweetest voice and smiled at Dad.

"Daddy, may we go see Little O now? All of our chores are finished," I said sweetly, glancing up into his eyes.

Frowning as his eyebrows pinched together, Dad hesitated, rubbing his hand on his chin. "It's your call, Gita. Is there time to go see that orangutan again?"

"*Ibu, ya,* please, I want see him." Zaqi soared with enthusiasm. "And *Ibu,* we read orangutans love durian. We buy for him?"

"*Ya,* good time. Buy durian Mr. John?" She grinned at Dad with her gentle eyes.

The corners of my mouth curled up into a big smile. What could be better than feeding Little O? I loved this day.

But Dad, always interested in proper protocol, brought up the scariest question. "Should we speak to the owner first? Maybe he's inside the store? Let's go in."

No way! I never told anyone about Maniac Man, that he beat Little O, that he grabbed my hand and that he tried to steal me. No way was I stepping foot inside that store.

Zaqi caught my troubled look, threw on his imaginary superhero cape, and spoke to his mom in Bahasa. Gita looked from Zaqi to me, noticing a problem. Dad, on the other hand, remained oblivious.

"*Ya?* Mr. John, you stay with Missy Jaylynn? Keep safe."

While Gita and Zaqi went into the store, I snuggled up next to Dad.

"It's hard to believe all that has happened since we first came to the market four days ago." I nuzzled even closer.

Obviously pulled out of his daydream, Dad wrapped his arm around me.

"You're right, honey. Things move fast here. I can't believe you want to feed that orangutan. It's dangerous with his sharp teeth." He rubbed my back while we stood quietly together.

After a long wait that seemed like an eternity, Gita and Zaqi walked over. From the serious look on Gita's face, I figured she had heard bad news. "Shopkeeper say orangutan for sale. He discover in rainforest wandering with no mother."

Zaqi jumped in to help his mom tell the story. "He say something happen to her because mother never leave young alone. He grab baby, or it die out in the jungle."

"He sell orangutan for 4,100,000 Rupiah. I bargain for you. *Ya?*"

"Yes, Dad, yes! That's the answer!" I cried. "Please Dad, buy the orangutan. I can love him. He won't be so lonely and miserable."

"Young lady, do you think money grows on trees? 4,100,000 Rupiah is about $300! Ridiculous! Besides, this conversation isn't concerning a dog or a cat, but a wild orangutan. We can't keep a pet orangutan in the house. That's not fair to him or us. He'll grow up and want to be wild. He'll make a mess everywhere, and I don't even know what he eats!"

As my abdomen tightened, I shut my eyes tightly to stop tears from falling. When I peeked out, Gita was watching me with her calm warm eyes. But hold it, I remembered, he had told Bima $200. What was up with that? Bima was right. We couldn't trust him. Time to tell the guys about Maniac Man and set this straight.

"Man say okay feed him," Gita said rubbing my shoulder.

Exhaling loudly, Dad's face strained trying hard to be patient.

Zaqi jumped in with his super smile. "We feed him durian and watch him eat. *Ya?* He hungry."

I glanced at Dad and he looked back at me, with a bewildered look on his face. He sighed one giant sigh and crossed his arms in front of his chest. Maybe Dad had gone through some weird changing machine when he moved here. Now instead of a marshmallow filling, he had thorns, thistles and broken glass. As if squeezing the words out from some tight spot within, he agreed to buy two durians.

Wanting to get my way, I chose to be uber polite. "So, you alright with watching us, but staying close to make sure we're safe?"

Dad agreed.

Zaqi walked right up to the orangutan, handed him the fruit and then plopped down onto the dirt. When I joined, sitting cross legged in front of Little O, yellow filled my heart, and I smiled a smile that started in my toes. "Little O, I love you!" I bundled every bit of yellow and shot it out of my heart, aiming at Little O.

Zaqi and I sat motionless, watching in amazement as Little O used his very strong jaws to crack the shell, and then pounded it into the dirt to split it in two, before gobbling it down. Overwhelmed by the horrific smell, my fingers squeezed my nose shut. "He looks like you eating that durian."

"*Ya*, like me, right. When hits tongue, whole body melt into happiness" Zaqi said in agreement.

We both giggled as we watched him and gave each other high fives, happy to help.

"He must be starving. Look how fast he's eating."

After Little O scooped out every morsel of durian from the shell, he looked me straight in the eye.

"Jaylynn, he want yours."

Not waiting for me to hand it to him, Little O climbed into my lap and I wrapped my arms around him. Little O opened the durian while I kept my nose sealed and took small shallow breaths to keep from being asphyxiated. Well, at least I'd die happy.

Maybe he's not getting any food. Last night he snarfed down bananas and now the durian, but he eats like he's starving. Did Maniac Man feed him anything? "Enjoy your durian. Guess it tastes as good as rocky road ice cream to me. Hey, think Little O might be my cousin? Our hair matches."

"Cousin?" Zaqi cracked up. Undisturbed by his laughter, Little O kept eating.

"Hey, watch his toes move, like fingers. So cool."

Watching him savor the durian as he rolled his eyes with each taste, I pictured eating an Oreo, slowly twisting off the top, dipping it in milk and then the good part, licking off the creamy filling.

Little O had the same concentration on his face as his fingers dug into the fruit, and then pure bliss when a glop of durian entered his mouth. That one moment of sensation when scrumptious tastes brought only one sound… mmm. His eyes filled with ecstasy as he exhaled a long-contented sigh.

"Hey, remember reading that they have the same number of teeth as humans?"

"*Ya*. Hey, he my cousin. Look at eyes, same color and look how he eat durian!" Zaqi laughed and waggled his eyebrows at me.

Before long we were laughing continuously, while Little O kept eating, not bothered at all by our antics. But then Zaqi's face twisted to serious.

"It very big thing sit close to orangutan. It honor. I see only photos. To feed him dream. *Terima kasih*. Thank you, Jaylynn. I help free. Team Little O Rescue."

"I can't believe you'll help me. *Terima kasih*. I can't do this myself without even speaking the language. Do you remember how much he told Bima? Wasn't it only $200 and now its $300? What's up with that?"

"He change price. I not know why."

"Bima is right. We can't trust him. Wouldn't it be easier to steal him? I'll be lucky if I can get $200."

Zaqi's face turned serious. "No steal. You get. You *Wani*."

Not believing either me or Wani could gather $200, I decided to keep taking money out of Dad's wallet. My little secret. When Little O's eyes met mine, a lightness formed inside me like a big balloon of love. My whole world, my heart, filled with yellow love. "It's not so bad to be in Sumatra instead of Seattle, if I can be with Little O," I said softly.

But quickly the deep sound of an adult's voice broke the magic spell.

"Kids, you fed him, and he liked it. Sweet to watch you both but now it's time to go home."

Sending Little O buckets of yellow, I gently moved him off my lap. Inside this voice spoke clearly, *Be brave now.* And then again. *No tears.* Nodding my head in silent agreement with the mysterious voice, I whispered, "We'll be back. Be brave. Zaqi and I will figure out how to get you back to the rainforest."

And Zaqi nodded his head in agreement to our secret pact to save Little O.

CHAPTER 16

NIGHT FIVE

After dinner, I found Zaqi parked at the computer with an orangutan site pulled up. "What did you find?"

"Orangutan be extinct soon. No rainforest. Palm oil destroy rainforest. Here read."

After a few clicks, as I read, I bit my lower lip. "Palm oil? Doesn't make sense. They demolish the rainforest, take down all the trees, and turn it into a palm oil plantation, which destroys the orangutan habitat, actually all the creature's habitat like the tigers and birds and elephants, leaving them nowhere to live. That's why they're endangered. Who needs palm oil? First, we save Little O and then we figure out how to save the rainforest."

Zaqi grinned at me. "You not cry now. You *Wani*."

"Dude. This page says orangutans could become extinct in the wild within the next five to ten years. No time for tears. They need help now!"

"How come no one know big nature problem? I not know."

"I never heard of it. But this says palm oil mixes into everything that we buy at home: baked stuff, chocolate, soap, shampoo, cereal, ice cream. And more… makeup, cleaning stuff, detergents and toothpaste. That's like… everything!"

"Why use palm oil if bad for rainforest? And orangutans?"

"Look up Crest toothpaste." There it was, on the list. "Try Dreyer's ice cream." Yes again. Totally depressing." I pounded the desk yelling, "Darnit. Darnit. Darnit."

Dad walked in with a puzzled look on his face. "What's all the ruckus?"

"Palm oil."

"Never heard of it."

A sigh escaped. "I'm so sad. Here, read this website and tell us why they're obliterating a perfectly good rainforest, killing orangutans to make palm oil? Can you help us understand?"

Within minutes Dad read it all and a dark curtain dropped in front of his face like the grocery store ran out of ice cream. Then he pushed out an exhale that sounded like a giant balloon poked by a pin. "Very interesting what you two have found. I've never heard anything about any of this before, but I'll research more on this matter later. At first glance, it's an economics issue. There's a resource, the rainforest, and that's like saying there's a pot of gold," he continued. "Leveling the rainforest to sell the wood makes someone money. Someone gets part of the pot of gold. And then they plant, then sell the palm oil and that's more money. It's very complicated to explain."

My brain muddled, my stomach twisted, and tears started to form, but I forced them to freeze. "But, shouldn't they care about their rainforest and all the plants and animals? Orangutans will be extinct if no one stops palm oil."

"*Ya*, why no care about orangutan?" From the look on his face, Zaqi's stomach hurt too.

"Kids, I want to explain this, so you understand." He looked away, straightened up in the chair and took a deep breath. "From your viewpoint, you care about the rainforest and the wildlife."

Unable to stop the pout, I folded my arms across my chest. "And Little O!"

"Yes, and Little O, too, but that pot of gold controls the choices people make all over the world. Companies in the United States and Europe and Asia buy palm oil and the rainforest wood. Resources from one place in the world supply products for another part. Money is exchanged. Now that's not to say you're helpless with no point of action." He rubbed his hands together like a magician promising a solution to appear any second. "Conservation groups exist, I'm certain. You two could research that next and find out how to help orangutans. With school beginning on Monday, you two could start a conservation club."

"But right now, people from Indonesia work and make money on palm oil plantations. It's their livelihood. And some big industries from all over the world make lots of money selling palm oil, using it in their products, like Crest, Dreyer's, Nestle and many more and that's always tough to stop."

My heart pounded. Tough to stop? As I held my breath looking from the computer to Dad then to Zaqi, I willed myself to stay strong. "But what about this palm oil stuff? Back home we ate things and used things that had palm oil in it. With not even a clue that it destroyed a rainforest and the orangutan's survival, too. Every time I brushed my teeth, a tree fell. Somehow, I'm like connected to orangutan extinction, but I didn't have an inkling. I feel so bad. What other products made that list?"

Dad looked at me with softness. "You two learned something here that's a black hole to a lot of grownups. Something they don't know about, either. Connecting what we buy with where we get the resources and how it affects the environment. Sustainability. And honestly, I never linked the two together. The truth remains that a connection exists between what we buy and where we get its ingredients. But stay away from gloom over this. Like I said, it's a pot of gold, it's been going on forever, and that's how people make money."

No one spoke. Bewildered, trying to sort it all out, I wondered how to change something that had been going on forever in the grownup world. Economics and this stupid pot of gold? Whatever. They only cared about money.

Gita walked in smiling. "All three sad, what wrong? Why quiet?"

Zaqi looked up at his mom. "*Ibu*, I sad. We learn pot of gold fell rainforest and kill all orangutans."

She tilted her head, her eyebrows lifting. "I not understand. Pot of gold?"

Zaqi explained it all to her in Bahasa, and her face joined ours in sadness.

Gita rubbed his back. "You and Missy Jaylynn friends

96

with Little O. Now what do? Worry, feel bad, not good. You fight for what you believe. You help." She looked us in the eyes with a clear message. If Little O had no mother to help him, we needed to act.

Zaqi stiffened, silent for a long time and then he spoke. "But, we two kids. Mr. John say this how world go. How we change world?"

Gita responded "My English not good. I try. You find problem, you find answer. *Ya?* Only bad pretend no problem. You find Little O, piece of big problem. *Dimana ada kemauan, di situ ada jalan. Ya?*"
"*Ya, Ibu.*

My frustration loomed. "Can you tell me what that means?"

"If you want do something very much, then you find way," Gita said.

Flashing on an image of Little O tied up, all alone, sending him yellow, wanting to solve his problem, and searching for a way to rescue him even if it was complicated. Gita put her arm around my shoulder, smiling her irresistible smile.

"Come here." Gita opened her arms wide. "Look at sad face." Touching my face right along the deep worry line on my forehead, she smoothed it out. "Hug. *Ya?*"

Not waiting one second for a happy, warm hug, I turned into her open arms.

"All work with orangutan. We no see answer now but *ya* believe."

Encircled in Gita's arms, a gentle hand stroking my hair, I relaxed. "Dad take good care, love you. I here, friend, and

Zaqi, too."

With that hug, I remembered my dream and how nothing could hurt me with Auntie's arms around me, protected. Gita's arms wrapped around me gave me the same shelter. Safe and relaxed, questions jumped out of my mouth before I could keep them inside.

"How can we save Little O? Dad won't help me. Little O's at the market, alone, not safe, hungry. I want to protect him and find his mother." My head dropped to her shoulder.

Gita rubbed my back making soothing sounds. "You heart tie with baby orangutan. Good. Help wild animal free. Missy Jaylynn have faith. Trust your heart."

"My mom says I'm strong and to make a plan, but how?"

Grabbing my face between her hands, Gita looked straight into my eyes. "Be patient. Not sad. *Ya?* You love life. Believe, little one. You on path. It is your fate. We say that the way deal with fate mark who we become. Not worry. You on right path."

Gita held me, and her words sank in. Saving Little O. My fate? What was that? My heart. All connected somehow.

"Little O wants his mom. Like me." That reality brought the tears. Embarrassed but comforted by her tight hug.

"*Ya.* You find way. Have patience and all will come. We not know how but answer come. Believe."

I gave Gita a hug and decided that I needed to Skype Matt. After a quick long distance hello, I told him all about palm oil.

"What else?" he asked. "You're twirling your hair."

Tears sprouted fast and rolled down my face, but I wiped them off quickly. "Things have changed. Still stealing from Dad's wallet because I want to be able to buy him but seems like it's better to sneak out and steal Little O. Tonight."

Matt's mouth dropped open, his eyes as wide as saucers. "What?"

After I explained that Maniac Man had told Bima $200 and told Gita $300, he understood. Of course, my two failed attempts to steal him didn't go over well either.

"What is happening to you there? It's totally crazy! You'd NEVER sneak out in Seattle or lie to your dad or even think of stealing. I'm so jealous."

I shrugged and sighed.

"But you couldn't even get past the dog the first time and had to sprint to barely escape Maniac Man the second time. What's different this time? How can you get him off the chain AND not get caught by Maniac Man AND get Little O back into your house AND keep him a secret from your dad?" Shaking his head, Matt said, "Really scary. Take Zaqi. Or don't do it."

"Zaqi won't steal or sneak out. There's no other way."

"Well, your name is Wani and can't imagine anything more daring! Just think you need to wait. Follow the plan. Dang, I wish I was there to help. Gotta go. Good luck!"

"Thanks!"

I slouched back in my seat but straightened up when Zaqi returned. Had he heard me say I wanted to sneak out? Afraid to make him mad, I kept my mouth shut. Once

Little O was here, he wouldn't be mad anymore. I bit my lip, my nerves getting the best of me.

"You not good? You bite lip. What wrong?" he asked.

"Afraid about collecting money. How's the driving coming?"

Zaqi smiled at me. "Driving easy. English hard. You help me?"

"Yes, you help me too. Bahasa Indonesia is tough for me."

After we practiced some phrases, I slipped off to my room, to wait till everyone fell asleep and I could sneak out, but when my head hit my pillow, I was out. The last thing I thought about before falling asleep was Little O flying through the rainforest on his mom's back.

CHAPTER 17

NIGHT FIVE
CONTINUES

What was I doing now in my school uniform but no
shoes? Where was my lunch? Was I late? When I looked
down, my feet were planted in moss and above me was an
enormous umbrella of branches, vines, and leaves. Bird
songs filled the air as they twisted down to earth like falling
leaves. "There must be like a million different birds all
having a concert at the same time, whistling and trilling like
flutes."

The invisible symphony played high above me. If I
stretched my neck, letting my head fall back, my eyes peered
through the spaces between the leaves that were painted
a million different shades of green, but not one bird was
visible. Sunlight filtered down through the maze of leaves
reminding me it was daytime. Everything shimmered
in serene light with little beads of water sparkling like
diamonds. The air here felt damp and alive.

Neon bright palm trees with vines winding around their
trunks hung low in front of my face. Branches swayed in
the slight breeze, a vine brushed my ear, a mosquito buzzed
by and a big brown scary looking bug crawled over my

foot making me jump. "Yuck! Too many bugs!" With both hands, I swatted at them.

"How am I going to get back home?" Scratching my head, the mystery of what I was doing in the rainforest continued. "Green plants everywhere but no trail leading out, only a thick blanket of moss-like carpeting. If I stop for five minutes, I'll be completely covered in bugs, moss, and vines!"

Suddenly a loud rumble like distant thunder jolted me and my eyes scanned every which way for trouble. *What made that loud commotion?* As I squinted to see through the dense, low leaves covered by a misty haze, my imagination went wild. Then the sound of branches breaking and leaves rustling, terrified me. Big limbs wobbled high above, loud rustling, with breaks of sunlight in the gaps. What kind of monster ripped through the forest? For a split second, in between two branches, something that looked like Sasquatch appeared. *What?* My mouth dropped open. *Impossible.* Ducking behind a giant tree no longer worried about snakes or bugs, I crouched down real low. *Yikes, am I dinner? Stay still. Stay quiet.*

Now the commotion came from right over my head. Barely breathing, I slowly lifted my eyes. Swinging on vines like an acrobat, it floated on air gracefully sailing through the forest. Enormous. And then I saw the color—orange, and hairy. *An orangutan?* Coming right for me. Shocked and petrified, hiding my face in my hands, too terrified to look, I almost peed my pants when it landed gracefully in front of me standing on its hind legs. I hid my face in my hands, too terrified to look.

"No need to be alarmed, little one. You know me."

What was she talking about? How could I know her? But that felt like yellow.

"You went to see Little O again. This time you fed him. You helped him."

Yellow filled my heart. I peeked between fingers. "Auntie? You send yellow, too?"

"Yes. Only you feel color because you friend to Little O. Climb on my back. I'll bring you to my nest where you'll be safe."

I hesitated, uncertain. But then green came through and I wanted to fly through the forest. It was cool to be doing the color thing with her too.

"But last time there were gun shots. Why were there gun shots Auntie?"

"Men come to kill mother orangutan to steal baby. Bad men. You know one. But safe now. Come here. You'll like it."

Cautiously scrambling up her back, her fur tickled my bare legs. Wrapping my legs and arms around her body for another hairy, scratchy, piggy back ride. No use pretending that I wasn't scared stiff. My heart beat so loudly I heard it in my ears. Breathing loudly, panting, both afraid and amazed.

"Don't be scared. Don't look down. There is no danger because I'll protect you."

And with that she swung on a vine and when she let go, off we flew, sailing through the air till she grabbed another and swung again. We kept sailing through the rainforest, my face nuzzled in her back flying higher and higher, from vine to vine. Little O must love these rides and how he must miss his mom. Finally, we landed on top of a tall tree near her nest, woven with branches, leaves and vines, nestled between two big limbs, hidden in a thick canopy of leaves.

"Come little one, shimmy off my back and curl up in my nest. I'll guard you. Go to sleep and rest. You'll be the champion for Little O. You'll bring him back to the rainforest."

"I want to rescue him. I do. But it's so much money… so much money…"

My eyes barely stayed open as the nest swayed gently in the breeze and the birds sang a lullaby.

Just before drifting off, Auntie said one more thing. "The money will come. Do not worry. But if not, you must steal him. Yes. Steal him. You know your job. Never give up."

CHAPTER 18

DAY SIX

That morning, we met up with Bima. He stood with a cocky grin on his face and a devilish look in his eyes, leaning on his scooter—our escape vehicle for Little O's rescue. Cool.

"*Sepupu*, you drive us. Get behind me *Wani*, and hold tight."

"Wait a sec." Time for the truth about Maniac Man and that first day. I explained everything to them. They both listened intently and held their breath when I got to the part about how he beat Little O. Both boys clenched their fists and when they started to speak, I held up my hand.

"Wait. There's more." When I described Maniac Man grabbing me, Bima flew over the edge, ferocious with anger, shouting, yelling and hitting his fist into his palm. Looked like war to me.

"Like I say. NOT trust this man. NOT buy Little O. NO! Steal him!" Bima said.

Zaqi took in a deep breath shaking his head sadness in his eyes. And it was all my fault dragging him into this rescue. "We steal. I not help."

Silence all around.

"We're a team and we all have to stick together. Can we think about it overnight? Let's go for a practice spin. Zaqi tells me he can drive this thing. Okay?"

Bima started to speak, to disagree but he pursed his lips and stayed quiet. Zaqi kept his thoughts to himself, too. Uncertain how we three would work this out, pressure mounted on me to get enough money. Otherwise, either Zaqi or Bima was going to be mad and maybe refuse to help. The whole mission would fail.

Zaqi revved up the engine, put on the gas and the scooter lurched forward. As if my life depended on it, my arms wrapped around Bima. Where would Little O sit? Could I keep him safe using only one arm? Would Little O be freaked out from all the noise? I buried my head in Bima's back.

The ride around town zigged and zagged as Zaqi swerved around cars and zoomed past other scooters. At first my arms were rigid but then they loosened up as I got more confident. But when a tight turn around a sharp corner made the scooter skid, both arms automatically locked around Bima's skinny body, probably cutting off his circulation.

Bima shouted orders continually as honking cars whizzed past us. Zaqi veered left to miss a motorcycle that came within a hair of hitting us. We all leaned away, almost tipping, and forced a lady crossing the street to jump out of the way.

Then out of nowhere a car swerved right in front of us. Bima roared, "*ZAQI, PELAN - PELAN! KAMI CRASH!*

But the warning came too late. *SCREECH!* My eyes sealed closed. Zaqi braked hard, slamming me into Bima's back. When the scooter's wheels locked, my body lurched backwards almost tearing my grip from Bima. Horns blasted, people yelled, tires squealed. When I opened my eyes, the chaos all around me forced me to shut them fast. My dad would kill me if we ended up in the hospital with casts on our arms and legs.

The scooter leaned left barely upright but Bima saved us by moving his shoulders back to the center. A becak screeched on his brakes to avoid smashing into us. Zaqi braked again, forcing the scooter to spin out. We were facing the wrong direction! Zaqi aimed toward the safety of the sidewalk but we hit a pothole dead on.

SWAAPFT! THWACK! The scooter skidded wildly out of control. As we spun out barely avoiding a car, the sound of squealing tires and bleeping horns filled the air. *KWA-WOMPUN! CRUNCH!* The scooter crashed. My body lifted off the seat, flying. With my arms wrapped around my head, my body hit the pavement. *THUD! OUCH!* Luckily landing on my side, my body skidding against the asphalt.

Hands, knees, legs, arms, all my bare skin burned as the pavement tore through it. When I opened my eyes, nasty little rocks on the street stared me in the face. Rubbing my head, which was still in one piece, dirt and stones scattered. After I rolled over on my back, someone smiled down on me, helping me sit up.

"*Apakah kamu baik baik saja? Apakah kamu baik baik saja?*"

Not a clue what that meant, I grinned. "*Terima kasih.*"

I then tried to spot the guys through the crowd. The scooter lay on top of Zaqi, its wheels spinning. People ran from everywhere to help him and lift the scooter.

Bima was not far from me, rubbing his shoulder. He had blood, lots of blood, dripping from his head onto his arm. Totally gross but he seemed okay.

"Bima?" I whispered. "You're a bloody mess. How bad are you hurt?"

"I fine. You?"

"Just cuts, scrapes, lots of little rocks. Heads still attached."

Bima shouted, "Zaqi, Zaqi you hurt?" Zaqi didn't reply and didn't move. He lay motionless on the pavement. I bit my lip, so afraid that he was dead. Slowly Bima stood up, rubbing his hip and limped over to his cousin. Scared about Zaqi, I stumbled towards them both. When I got to Zaqi, my knees collapsed. His eyes were shut. *Please. Please. Let him be alive.*

Bima rested his hand on Zaqi and spoke to him in Bahasa. I held his hand not knowing what else to do. Zaqi finally opened his eyes that weaved in circles like bumblebees buzzed inside his head. "*Kau anak baik-baik saja?*" Bima said. "No time for joking. You hurt?"

Zaqi laid his hand on his head. "My whole head throb." He sat up and tried to get up, but his knees buckled, and he flopped back down. His head rolled around like it might fall off. "My head spin."

Sitting on the pavement, inspecting the cuts on the side of my leg, a real mess for certain. A pretty good patch of skin was torn up, red, bleeding with bits of dirt and gravel ground inside. The palms of my hands burned and looked awful. More gravel and dirt stuck inside those scratches. I tried blowing on my hands to cool them off. "What a wipe-out-your-skin sort of crash. What's up with Zaqi? Did he hit his head? Does he have a concussion?"

Zaqi braced his head in his hands, not noticing the blood dripping from his arm. "The scooter. I wreck? Bima, I sorry."

"Hey, *sepupu*, wipe blood off. Scooter fine." He smiled. "Big thunder crash. Congratulations! You live through first smash up." Bima used his shirt to clean up his cuts and was seemingly not very worried at all. "You guys are covered in blood. What will your moms say? What shall I tell my dad? He'll kill me." Tenderly, I brushed off my leg trying to pick out some of the bigger stones from my palm.

"Tell him you fell playing soccer after school."

I ran that through my lie detector. Not a bad idea. "He's pretty distracted these days. He might believe me." When I walked around testing out my legs, no limp. "But there's going to be a giant black and blue where I landed," rubbing my hip. "That was absolutely crazy!"

"And me? Bima, what tell *Ibu?*"

"The truth. Tell her you on back of scooter and we tip over. Not that we in crash. Not that you drive. Small lie." Bima smiled at both of us completely in control of the calamity.

"I not lie to *Ibu*. Never. I tell truth."

Shaking his head at his cousin, Bima let it go. "Hop on. I drive. I take scooter to friend for fix and then come to house. All be fine."

CHAPTER 19

DAY SIX
CONTINUES

At home, after picking most of the little stones out of my palms, shins, and arms, I headed out to the swings, now known as Command Central. Everything was debated or resolved there. Zaqi's injuries were way worse than mine. "They hurt?"

"No, not hurt. I deserve hurt. I drive bad. Hurt everyone." He shook his head looking glum. Zaqi squinted at my injuries. "I sorry. You hurt. My fault. Bad driver."

With a sense of pride, I checked out all of my cuts and scrapes. "Hey, it's cool and I'm fine. Warrior wounds. Why feel bad? The scooter still drives. I like my new cuts and Dad believed me when I said it was from a soccer tackle. These are medals for courage and bravery in the line of duty."

Zaqi smiled. "You very brave, *Wani*."

"I don't know about that. Next up, me on money. Talk about goofing up. But I know you don't want to steal him. Once we have the money, we need to buy Little O from Maniac Man. Let's ask Bima to negotiate."

"*Ya?* Bima good. But we not bring Little O home. We drive rainforest."

"Maybe Bima knows which road to get to the rainforest? We need gas money, too."

Bima walked over from the gate, interrupting our conversation. "Scooter all good for trip. When you two leave?"

I shrugged. "If we have the money, next Friday? I need to talk to Matt. He must know how to get his money here because I don't have a clue. On Friday, Dad will be at work. Should we, like, leave a note?" I knew not to say anything about taking money from Dad's wallet, which would make Zaqi mad and he'd quit the team."

"Maybe? Not want them believe you kidnapped," Bima said.

"Oh, my gosh! And call the cops," I said.

"*Ibu* scared," Zaqi said.

Silence fell between us like a heavy curtain. My grip tightened on the swing chains, pressing the metal into my palms. Truthfully, I'd never disobeyed my parents before and now look at me. The deeper we got into the rescue, the more rules we violated. By the time Rescue Day arrived, juvenile detention would be a short hop away for sneaking out, stealing money, ditching school, and then add in making Bima and Zaqi help me steal an orangutan. A pretty wild path, with tons of defiant, rule-breaking activities. But what if those bad things meant a good thing happened? The way I saw it, Little O had a right to live in the rainforest. That counted for something, didn't it?

Bima remained quiet. What might he be thinking to make him silent? Guess he had a lot to worry about. He felt responsible for our safety. His scooter could get wrecked, after all. What would happen if Maniac Man stopped us? Or worse, my dad? I watched him brood, wondering why he even bothered to help us. Guess he loved Little O, too?

Zaqi bore the death watch on his face, chock full of uneasiness, with no hints of his usual grin. I'd forced him into this predicament. My best friend here and I'd twisted him into Mr. Miserable. Didn't need to be a brain surgeon to know what bugged him the most. His mom, the coolest mom ever, and now he'd lied to her and slipped around her, stuff he'd never done before I moved here. If she discovered the truth, she'd be mega-disappointed.

Everyone behaved badly now because of me. "I feel terrible. I had no idea how much danger you guys would be in. If you don't want to help anymore, I'd totally understand."

Zaqi gave me an 'are you nuts?' look. "What about Little O? What happen to him?" Zaqi asked. "I love Little O. I want rescue him. I never call off."

Bima took in a deep breath. "Freedom for Little O important. But steal Little O. Man not trust. Everything be fine after Little O free."

"NO steal. I NO DO. We buy. I NO steal." Zaqi crossed his arms across his chest as a frown smeared his face. "I NO help."

Silence. Nothing from Bima and not a peep from me. I needed Zaqi to drive. And he was my friend. How to solve this? Whichever action I took, Gita said it determined my character. If I turned my back on Zaqi, he'd never forgive me. We'd never be friends again. If I lied to my dad and Gita and Zaqi, but saved Little O? What if the only solution was to steal Little O? Wasn't that all fate Gita told me about? Now, to keep my friend, I needed to figure out how to collect money no matter how much easier stealing seemed.

Back at the house, I Skyped Matt to tell him every little detail about my latest dream and the cool part about our crash. I showed him my hands and elbows all scraped up, red, and ugly.

"You were in a crash? Dude. I'm like so jealous. You have all the luck. And your dad hasn't caught on to any of this? Even with your scraped legs and hands? No way. And you dreamt about Auntie. What does it mean if she said not to worry about money?"

"She must know something because right now it's just my change and the money I've been taking from Dad's wallet."

"What if he notices? You're gonna get caught and get grounded for like forever. Jaylynn you're a real live juvenile delinquent. You're so lucky. You guys have all the fun! Scary guys to deal with and buying Little O... Get on it, Wani! No more stalling. I can't wait to hear about that. I started collecting donations yesterday. Hope to get a lot."

"But Bima thinks we should steal him. He doesn't trust Maniac Man. But Zaqi will quit the gang if we steal him."

"I get that. Steal him? Get caught? I better collect money faster to keep you guys out of jail!" Matt rubbed his hands together, fired up.

CHAPTER 20

NIGHT SIX

At dinner that night, Gita told us about a special store that stocked American food. "We go tomorrow. *Ya?* What you say?"

"OMG, really? What a great idea!" I exclaimed. I couldn't believe my luck. "I'd love that grocery store. Let's get peanut butter and jelly, white bread, macaroni and cheese, and Cheerios, too." My mouth watered as I pictured some favorites.

Zaqi crunched up his face into a quizzical look. "What peanut butter and jelly? And Cheerios?"

"Dude! Wait until you taste a bowl of Cheerios, like, it's so good with cold milk and bananas. And macaroni and cheese, too. I hope they stock it at the store. You can taste some of my food. Can't wait to make PB and Js!"

"I happy go store buy American food." Gita, my fairy godmother, smiled and winked at me. Hope she knew how much I appreciated her help. I grinned at Dad.

"Can we go see Little O after grocery shopping?"

"That's up to Gita since I'll be at work. Because school starts tomorrow, make sure that is your priority."

"*Ya*, after school, we shop and then go see. I like Little O, too." Gita winked at me and smiled at Zaqi.

"I can't wait to shop tomorrow. Can I be excused?" I squealed.

Back in my room, I bounced onto my bed, eyes opened wide staring at the ceiling fan.New school, new kids, new teachers, and money. But how could I be the new kid, tell the girls at my lunch table about Little O and ask them for money? What if no one sat with me? Thoughts of home flew around my mind. The only thing the same here as in Seattle was my underwear! Hope no one teased me about my freckles or my red hair. Worries buzzed around my head like angry hornets. What the heck?

Dad walked into my room right in the middle of my thick twist of thorny thoughts. "Honey, ready for bed? Big day tomorrow. School, then shopping for American food! I bet you have a great first day." Since I didn't answer him, he paused for a minute and tussled my hair.

After I flipped over and raised myself up on my elbows, my head hung low, but I swallowed down tears, determined not to cry.

"Tell me. What's wrong?"

"I'm a wreck. About school. Worried. How can I fit in here? It's like a whole new country!"

"If anything makes you unhappy at school, come right home and tell me about it, Jaylynn. We'll find a way to solve the problem together," he said trying to soothe me.

Looking out the window at the palm tree swaying in the night breeze, I bit my lip.

"But there's more?"

"I miss everything from Seattle, like cool breezes, evergreens, the food, and especially my friends." I managed to leave Mom off that list, even though I missed her the most.

"Right on that. Me, too. I miss salmon barbeques. But give it some time. We just arrived here, and things will get a lot better. It will be okay. I promise." Dad hugged me, and I leaned my head against his shoulder, sleepy and safe.

"It seems like forever since we lived in Seattle. How could it only be six days?"

"By the end of the week you'll have new friends at school," he told me. "And a trip to the new grocery store will help. It's no use taking up too much time worrying."

"The store is great news. I can't eat any more rice." I sucked in that grumble as fast as I could, but the words had already escaped my lips. Twirling my hair between my fingers, I scolded myself—hating to complain about anything involving Gita, my fairy godmother. At least I'd managed to hold off my flood of questions about Mom.

Dad eyeballed me, and our eyes connected. "Buy whatever you want at the new grocery store," he replied. "Load up!"

"Really? If I find anything from home, I'll buy all of it! Thinking about mac and cheese makes my mouth water. The only thing that makes this move bearable is Little O. Lucky, I stumbled upon him. He helps me not miss home so much."

Dad sighed, clenching his jaw. "You and that orangutan. I wish I understood why you like him so much. We never even had a cat or dog at home."

He shook his head as a deep furrow formed on his forehead. Whenever I started talking about Little O, his mood changed to grumble, and he squinted, a bad sign for certain, his eyebrows drawing together until they nearly met. The deeper his squint, the deeper the trouble.

"But that's it. I always wanted a dog, but you and Mom never let me." I stopped to breathe.

"He won't now or ever be your pet. Get that straight. He's a wild animal sweetheart. Remember that."

I punched the pillow a couple of times. "No more talking. Good night."

Dad sat there for a moment, his face screwed up. He wrapped me up in his arms like a big strong bear. "My sweet girl, it will get better. For now, remember I love you. Now go to sleep. Tomorrow is your big day hunting for peanut butter! Sweet dreams, honey. Jaylynn?"

"What Dad?"

"I just noticed how bad these cuts and scrapes on your elbows and forearms are. What in the world really happened?" Alarm sounded in his voice as he held up my arms looking at all the cuts, obviously concerned. "Is this why you are upset? It's horrible looking. Sore too?"

Putting on my best though unpracticed lying face, taking one hand and rubbing it over the wounds. "Oh, these? It's nothing."

"I'm worried about you."

"Remember? I told you, soccer on the playground. It's cement here, not grass. This big kid at halfback, well, I didn't want the kids to think I was soft, let's just say I won't be charging anyone that big!"

Dad sighed, lifting his head to the sky and then wrapped me up in another hug. "Well please be careful or play on the grass for goodness sakes.""I'm fine. Time to sleep though."

"Good night honey."

With concern over what a good liar I was becoming, I drifted off to sleep.

CHAPTER 21

DAY SEVEN

I woke up blasting with enthusiasm and my hands shot up over my head. "YAAASSS! Let's get this mission moving." No time for grumbling about little things. Jumping out of bed, I fished around my backpack, my jeans, and my dresser drawers for loose change. I counted it all up—$14. Then I went to the pocket where I kept all the money stolen from Dad's wallet. So far, $87 total. I needed $113 more. What a loser. Matt told me to get help at school, but how could the new kid in town ask for money?

At breakfast, I poked Zaqi in an attempt to hurry him up, but his face told me to lay off.

"Let's hit the road. Time for school." I grabbed my backpack and went straight for the door not even stopping to hug Dad. He looked up from his paper and eyed me curiously.

"Feeling good about school, honey?"

Nodding and smiling, I managed to keep myself from rolling my eyes. Let him believe I liked school. Well, maybe I would.

Zaqi swallowed one more bite and once out the door,

gave me a puzzled look. "What hurry? Why?"

"I cooked up an idea. First, I'm going to tell the girls at my lunch table about Little O."

"What? Why? How can be? It not safe. You not know them."

"I have to. Matt started collecting money and I only have $113. I'm so lame. Plain and simple. I need money."

Zaqi walked silently, eyeing the cracks in the sidewalk, his hands in his pockets. "What happen if one of girls tell parents?"

True enough, I thought, if just one girl told a friend and that person told another friend, who told a parent, who told a teacher, who told my dad, everything would explode. *KABAM!*

"You're right. Risky to ask but I need help. Think Maniac Man will really sell him to us or cheat us like Bima thinks?"

Zaqi stayed quiet, not answering. His face reddened but still nothing. I walked faster as the schoolyard came in sight.

"Why you walk quick? What wrong?"

I spit it out machine gun speed, hating what I had to say. "If this money thing doesn't work, more and more it seems like we have to steal him. What else can we do?"

"I not steal. Not on team. I quit." Without even looking at me, he ran up the schoolyard steps, two at a time. He slammed his hands on the front doors shoving them open. Mad at me. All my fears slapped me like hail hitting a tin roof.

"Zaqi? Zaqi!" I hollered after him, but he ran away, speeding through the hall. Now what? My best friend, my only friend in Sumatra, was super angry and not speaking to me. Maybe at lunch he'd talk? What if he wouldn't drive the scooter? OMG, what a mess.

My first day at school surprised me because it seemed like a typical first day of school in Seattle with lots of introductions, directions, and assignments. Sitting in class, rescue daydreams and flying through the rainforest with Auntie drowned out the teachers' voices. Stealing Little O took front and center as I worked on How and When. Still I questioned whether to tell Bima and Zaqi all about Maniac Man. And what about my dream? Secret or tell?

As I sat through my morning math class, I could think of nothing but the rescue and how to do it without Zaqi. Our teacher, Mr. Selachi, a tall, bald man with a big belly, wore the same pair of suspenders every day, or so the kids said. The big moist rings that grew under his arms were totally gross. He was from England so he did speak with a cool accent, but math was still math. I purposely sat in the back row closest to the window in the hopes that Mr. Selachi wouldn't call on me ever. Worried about Zaqi, I slumped in my desk and glanced outside. Even though nothing great ever happened out there, it beat decimals by a long shot.

Right in the middle of my daydream, Mr. Selachi bellowed, "Jaylynn, get back here. Stop daydreaming!"

Startled, I about fell out of my chair and the whole class laughed. Slowly I straightened up, face as red as a beet not daring to look at anyone in the room.

"Quiet class!" Mr. Selachi yelled. Luckily the bell rang, and I flew out of there fast.

My next class, Bahasa Indonesia, dragged on, equally painful. My eyes darted to the clock every other minute. Fillino Tampubolon, patient and pretty, repeated everything slowly. She told us that she grew up in Aceh, in Northern Sumatra, close to Gunung Leuser, Little O's rainforest. She'd know all about how to get there. But, right now she said, "Repeat after me. Hello, *Selamat pagi* and thank you, *Terima kasih*."

My last class before lunch was my favorite, Daily News, with Mr. Grey, who wasn't grey at all, but young and handsome. Dark curly hair, with a straight nose, like a movie star. He knew how to dress, too. With blue eyes that twinkled, he never had to tell the class to be quiet. We girls paid attention to his every word. Even the boys respected him. Today he read an article about the rainforest, orangutans and palm oil and I answered many of his questions.

"Jaylynn, do you have a strong interest in orangutans? Would you like to do a report on the problems in their environment that cause their extinction?"

OMG, I had all his attention. Such dreamy eyes. I really wanted to impress him and tell him about Little O. Bet he'd know how to help. But if I said anything, I'd risk messing up Little O's rescue. Mom called this a pivotal moment, deciding which path to take. Time to lie to protect the rescue. Sorry, Mr. Grey.

"Yes, I can do a report. We have orangutans in the zoo in Seattle and I attended a talk there. I hope to see them here in the rainforest someday."

"They live in the Gunung Leuser rainforest, which

is about two hours from here." *What? Did he say Gunung Leuser, the same name from my dream? So, it was right.* Mr. Grey glanced out the window nodding his head slowly. "It's a gnarly problem full of conflict. Perhaps I'll consider arranging a field trip to see the wild orangutans and palm oil plantations. How many want to go there?"

Instantly, everyone's hand shot up in the air. Mr. Grey smiled and said he'd study it. When the bell rang, my classmates surrounded me, thanking me for bringing up orangutans. The very idea that they might like me because of my love for Little O amazed me and I floated on air all the way to the lunchroom full of pats on the back.

When I strolled up to Zaqi, I'd forgotten that he wasn't talking to me and when he turned away without a word, I was shattered. I'd never seen Zaqi mad and now the plan would fail. Replaying our conversation about stealing Little O, the problem jumped out. Rather than asking him, I'd told him we would steal Little O. Bad team player. Zaqi loved Little O and wanted him reunited with his mom. He also loved his mom and wouldn't hurt her. Who knew if he'd ever talk to me again?

At lunch the girls from my Daily News class giggled with each other and invited me to sit down. With my insides all wobbly, I smiled at Kari, barely a wisp of a thing from the U.K., with short blonde hair and braces. She busily pulled out crumpled sheets of paper from her backpack complaining about a misplaced assignment but slipped her arm out of her backpack for a high five. "Nice work! Very cool if we get a field trip in Mr. Foxy Grey's class. You really like orangutans?"

"Yes, definitely." I sat down next to her, pulling out my lunch.

"I've never seen one, not even at a zoo."

"Well, there's one at the market that I'm friends with."

All six of the girls at the table stopped gibbering and stared open-eyed at me. Guess I'd crossed the line with that last statement. Weemin, exactly my height and build, with straight black hair that I envied, perfect bangs and a very cool pair of glasses, gave me the look I dreaded—like I was nuts. When Weemin spoke, everyone listened. She asked what everyone else wondered.

"You said you're friends with an orangutan? Aren't they dangerous?"

"He's a little baby. Here, look for yourself." I grabbed my phone with the photo of Little O sitting on my lap and passed it around. "Took a selfie with him. He's mad wonderful and I love him so much."

The collective sounds of ooh and aah encouraged me, followed by a flood of questions, like why's he there, when do we get to see him, how often do I see him, and on and on. They were excited, and it seemed like a perfect time to begin. I took a deep breath and stopped because Zaqi was staring at me. If Zaqi said it was a bad idea, it was a bad idea. And the bell rang before I could tell them more or ask for help. "See you tomorrow," I said. Looked like that option failed. Well, maybe Matt would get lots of money. Out of the corner of my eye, I caught Zaqi staring at me with a curious look on his face. I smiled. *Come on, stop being mad*. But he turned and walked away.

After school, I ran to catch up with him.

"I owe you a big apology. It was thoughtless of me to act like some General in the army making all the decisions. I get that you are mad. We're a team."

Zaqi stared at me like fairy dust was sprinkled on my nose. "Ya. I mad. Not good steal."

"Well, then I better buy a ticket for the lottery! I don't know where $200 will come from."

Happy that he wasn't mad anymore we walked home exchanging stories about our classes. I promised to help him with his English homework if he'd help me with Bahasa Indonesia.

When we got home, Gita was ready to head out shopping. Gita's friend, who also worked for an American family, had told her to shop at Mr. Ben's on *Jl. Muara Takus*, a small store full of favorite American foods. On our walk there, I permanently glued every street and turn to my memory.

The instant we walked through the doors, all the jars and boxes and brands on the shelves screamed home. "Look, peanut butter! A big jar! And over there, strawberry jelly with plain old white bread for sandwiches. This store rocks!" I found a box of Cheerios but the best discovery? Oreos. "Dad loves these. He's going to be so happy!"

Maybe Gita had it right. Have some patience and things will all work out. Loaded down with grocery bags full of my favorite things, we walked over to the market to visit Little O. Gita walked inside the store to check with the owner about feeding Little O some durian but when she walked out, her usual smile had slipped behind a dark cloud.

"Jaylynn and Zaqi, store keeper say today someone buy

Little O. They no pay money but say come back."

Panicked, I held my breath, my hand covering my mouth. "NO! We're acting now. We can't let someone buy him."

Zaqi's face drained of blood, fear filled his eyes. "How to help? I not know."

We both fell silent wondering how to save Little O from becoming someone's pet. Gita watched us, but she'd run out of magic.

I shook my head, looking at the ground. "Dad won't let me buy him."

Gita hugged us drawing us in close. "Maybe man lie. He trick us."

My optimism nosedived. "How can we figure out if that shopkeeper lies?" I rubbed my head contemplating a plan. "How can we solve this? We'll tell him we'll buy him? We lie too?"

The usual sparkle in Gita's eyes vanished as she rubbed our backs. Something needed to happen fast or else we might lose our chance to set Little O free. It didn't seem like we had a week. Maybe we only had a day!

"Our most important thing, Little O," Zaqi said. "He hungry now. We feed him because that why we came, not worry about tomorrow."

Surprised to hear him take charge and be so certain, I eyeballed Zaqi. "I get it. Our mission now: feed Little O."

After we bought durian, we turned the corner and Little O scampered right up to us making a squeaky sound. He blinked slowly, a smile in his eyes, and I shot a band of yellow to the sweetest part of my life. No way was anyone buying him as a pet. My job needed to happen fast. Little O trusted me, and I had a responsibility. Maybe I could sneak out tonight and steal him. Then I could hide him in my room until Zaqi was ready to drive us. That could work. I examined the chain to look for that loose link. I'd need a tool.

While he ate his durian cuddled up in my lap, I clamped down hard on my nose to keep from gagging from the stench, which made Zaqi laugh. Holding my nose, I told Little O my latest dream, sleeping in his cozy nest and riding through the rainforest on his Auntie's back up to a nest. I told him that Auntie said I could steal him.

Zaqi listened to me and watched Little O. "No steal." Again, his anger rose to his face. "I not be orangutan rescue gang if steal."

Then, a lightning bolt of love hit me. This sweet baby orangutan made my heart warm. If I had no choice, I'd steal him with or without Zaqi.

"He understand you?" Zaqi said. "Look how he stare at you while you talk. Look at eyes. He trust you. Little O, we make plan get you back rainforest."

Little O twirled my hair with his fingers and nuzzled up against my shoulder, wrapping me tight with his other arm. I hugged him back, rubbed his arms, gently tussling his head like Gita and Auntie did for me, the same way, to give that love to Little O, to let him feel safe, even for a little while.

"I wonder if he could learn a high five. That would rock. High fiving an orangutan." I stopped mid-sentence, shocked by my words. How stupid am I? Little O belongs in the jungle living as a wild animal. He's not a pet, not my pet, learning dumb tricks. He belongs in the wild with his mom learning to swing from vine to vine. She'll teach him to find food and to build a nest. Little O belongs to the rainforest, to nature, not to me and not to any human.

"I know how scary living here without your mom is but be brave and have courage." I wondered what color I should send for bravery. Maybe silver like a knight's armor or gold like a magic shield. "Gita says that we might not know the way to solve this now but there is a way and we'll find it. Stay strong, sweet Little O. We'll come back soon."

I wrapped him up in a magic gold shield and hoped that it worked. What if someone came and bought him tomorrow? I wouldn't know where to find him. I had to steal him. No other way. But what about Zaqi?

"Little O," Zaqi said, "you no scare. *Aku mencintaimu.*"

"Wish I understood your language and what you said."

Zaqi looked at the ground and mumbled out of the side of his mouth, "I love you."

I grinned from inside out and whispered, "*Aku mencintaimu*, Little O."

Zaqi reached out his hand and touched fingers with Little O, who looked intently into his eyes.

CHAPTER 22

NIGHT SEVEN

Landing home from the market, I couldn't wait until 10 pm, which was 7 am in Seattle, to Skype Matt. I just wanted to hear his voice and to catch him up on all the Little O action, but when I sat at the table for American food night, everything slowed down. Dad and I dug in with a vengeance!

"This macaroni and cheese tastes amazing. And canned pears! Chips and dip!" Dad eagerly filled his plate for seconds. "Great job shopping and nice job cooking."

Dad and I dished up mountains of American food—raving over each taste, big smiles between every bite, until finally we lifted our heads like we finished a marathon. In contrast, Gita and Zaqi used their forks to take tiny bites. They had barely eaten anything. When I questioned Zaqi, he glanced at his mom with a quizzical look, shrugging his shoulders and rolling his eyes.

"Wait. American food tastes bad to you?" I grinned from ear to ear. "That's incredible."

"Chip good. Maybe with sambal me like" Zaqi remarked.

Gita smiled but hadn't eaten much. "New taste. Not know this flavor."

"I'm sorry, you two. Please eat what you like and leave the rest." Dad grinned at Gita, his eyes filled with kindness.

"No, it good. I not know this taste. What is?" Zaqi held up his fork holding the macaroni and cheese.

"We like cheese in America. Cheese on burgers, cheese on pasta, cheese on crackers, hot cheese on Doritos, grilled cheese sandwiches." I started to laugh. "But there's no cheese here. Peanut butter and jelly sandwich tomorrow. There's lots more things, too." I rolled my eyes in bliss.

"Ya, eat American food. Very new. Not know." Gita laughed, getting up from the table as she watched Dad and I scoop up ever last drop of food. "You like, *ya?*"

"Thank you for American night. Perfectly delicious! Jaylynn use the time after dinner to do your homework. No time for fooling around with anything else."

Luckily, Gita walked back in holding a plate brimming with Oreos, and Dad's face lit up.

"Oreos? Now we're talking!" He quickly popped one off the plate and straight into his mouth savoring the flavors, reaching for another one.

When Zaqi saw the plate of cookies, his eyes widened. "Oreos? American treat? Good, *ya?*"

"Yes! Yes!" I snatched one and started to twist off the top. "I need to teach you how to eat this. Never eat an Oreo whole. Twist, lick and dunk. Here's how." I held the top and the bottom and then very carefully twisted them in opposite directions without breaking either piece. "You try."

Both Gita and Zaqi carefully twisted off the tops of

their Oreos.

"Wait, Dad. Where's the milk?"

Dad walked into the kitchen and brought out four glasses of milk for me to complete my demonstration. "Now dunk each side into the milk. It's simple. Remember the magic words. T.L.D.E....Twist, lick, dunk and eat."

After their first bite, their grins widened like they were eating durian. "Good. I like this. American food good," Zaqi said. "I need another."

"I'll wash the dishes tonight." I smiled from ear to ear. "You really made my day with all this American food. Thank you."

Zaqi glanced over at me. His eyes twinkled. Maybe it was the sugar.

"Hey, you're wearing a milk mustache with Oreo crumbs. Now you look American." I dissolved into giggles as Zaqi walked to the mirror to check it out. American food night tasted great and even Dad seemed happy. Maybe Oreos were the missing medicine for him.

After I did the dishes and went back to my room to work on math, a horrible thought crossed my mind. What if palm oil was in Oreos? What the heck? Clicking on the computer, typing in 'palm oil in Oreos' knowing that I'd hate it if the answer was yes. "NO! That's not right! NO!" I shouted.

Dad flew into the room concern all over his face. "What's all the ruckus about?"

"Dad, you won't believe this. Palm oil made the ingredient list in Oreos. I can never eat another Oreo again. Orangutan extinction from Oreos? It's too crazy.

Goodnight!" I stomped off in frustration.

I knew it sounded stupid to be upset about an Oreo but I was miserable that something so good could be so bad for the rainforest. One thing for sure, once I got Little O back to the rainforest, palm oil would be my next battle.

When I awoke still in my clothes, it was the middle of the night and I jumped out of bed remembering my mission. Steal Little O. Tonight! No one else could buy him and end his chance at freedom. The clock said midnight. I ran down to the kitchen, grabbing bananas and the can opener—the only tool in the drawer—hoping maybe it would open the chain and free Little O.

Sneaking out of the house was a snap. Vision adjustments, tiptoeing, slithering and creeping, all skills gathered from the first two trips. I snuck past the guard, into the street with no dogs in sight. Cars and scooters and becaks zoomed around. Imitating a submarine, I lowered to hide behind bushes, duck behind trees, and every time I got spooked, I submerged and waited. During my time hidden, Little O received buckets of yellow.

Spotting a group of kids hanging out on the street corner, smoking cigarettes, and talking loudly, I hid behind a tree, trembling, my chest heaving, hoping they weren't some dangerous gang. I think my heart pounded loud enough for them to hear. I told myself it was all my imagination, but as fear grabbed my throat, I slid down the tree. They hadn't seen me yet, but if I left my hiding spot, I'd be in plain view.

Crouched there, full of dread, uncertain what to do, my courage materialized from deep within, throwing panic out into the darkness. Wani arrived. Slowly counting to ten, preparing myself to walk out, I stood up trying to get my thoughts in order.

But then someone grabbed my arm shocking the breath right out of my body. Their grip tightened on my wrist. Please don't let it be some bad dude or worse, Dad. My eyes rolled down slowly, heart racing. Time stopped. Was this how my life would end? My final minutes? I readied my foot to swing back and kick, then heard my name.

"Jaylynn. Shh…. It me. Zaqi," he whispered.

Looking up into his face, I almost collapsed. "What? You followed me? But your mom?"

"Time for talk later. You go Little O, *ya*? Follow me. Be fast, *ya*?"

But my plan was to steal Little O tonight. How could I tell him? We walked quickly but when the guys across the way saw us, they yelled something, which Zaqi ignored. When they followed us, Zaqi grabbed my hand and shifted our path toward a house. Heading to the back as if we lived there, we dashed behind a bush. My hands shaking. My knees wobbled and Zaqi motioned to me to calm down.

After a wait that lasted forever, he signaled that the coast was clear and we slipped away, darting through backyards toward the market. Every time I spoke, he told me to be quiet.

When we got to the market, we crept around towards Little O but sure enough, Maniac Man was standing near him with another man, speaking loudly. Maybe right before our eyes, someone was buying Little O. Little O sent red. Fear!

"Zaqi," I whispered, "What's going on? Is he selling

Little O? Zaqi put his finger up to his lips. How could I stay quiet? Then, feeling more red, I sent back yellow and whispered, "Zaqi, we have to stop this! Let's make noise, distract them, and break this thing up."

Zaqi grabbed my hand, keeping me down. "Jaylynn, they no talk about buy Little O. They talk about steal another baby from rainforest! Very bad men."

It took a few minutes to register. This stealing baby orangutans was like their business? Was this tied in to the shooting in my dreams? Should I tell Zaqi now? We needed to get Little O back to the rainforest and then shut Maniac Man down. Throw him into the slammer, jail, prison with a life sentence. "That's beyond terrible. We must stop them. Get Little O."

CHAPTER 23

DAY EIGHT

After school, I Skyped Matt. We kept interrupting each other until we both burst out laughing. "Okay, you go first." he said.

"In total, I have $102 from Dad's wallet. $14 of that is my own."

"What if he catches you?" Matt asked.

"Grounded for life. Or sent to boarding school."

"And to think you used to be so good. I let everyone see the photos you sent me and got $76! Let me add it all up. Yes! Only short $22."

Stunned, I stared into the screen. That much money? Remarkable! "So, how do you get the money to us?"

"I called Western Union and used my grown-up voice like this." Matt cleared his throat and deepened his voice, speaking slowly. "They said kids can wire money and pick it up. You need your passport. Know where it is?"

"Somewhere in Dad's desk, I guess. Unless it's locked in a safe."

"And a note from your dad. The way I figure, I'll wire you our money, and we'll help you save Little O from 8,000 miles away."

"Can they keep it secret? Won't everyone be talking about it?"

"Yeah, I really want to tell my parents." Matt's eyes grew big as he raised his eyebrows.

"If you tell your parents, absolutely they'll talk to Mom or worse, Dad. Then big trouble crashes on us." I winced picturing Dad's reaction. "Headline would read: New Transplant to Sumatra Gets Sent to her Room Forever."

"I see your point, but I've never hidden anything this big from them." Matt's eyes told me everything. Sneaking behind his parents' backs was a problem.

"You positive you're good helping? I get it if you'd rather not." No way did I sound sincere, because I really needed Matt's help for a whole lot of reasons.

"For sure. How can I leave Little O tied up and beaten? Only grounded for life if they catch me." Matt smiled, and I smiled back. "We're a long way from buying candy on the way home from school. Living large in Indonesia."

I bit my lip, my nerves getting the best of me.

"You nervous? You're biting your lip. What's wrong?"

To shake off the worries about getting caught, followed by a massive punishment, I thought about not returning him safely to the rainforest. Ultimately, I held the keys to his freedom. One baby orangutan either got freedom or ended up as a pet or worse, starved to death. "Parents schmarents. *Pffft…* Saving Little O is the most important thing. Who cares if they get mad for like forever? They can't send me to jail or give me to other parents."

Matt stopped talking. Finally, he said, "I'm in. Not

some whiny little kid here telling Mommy and Daddy. No way. We're going to save Little O!"

"Right! We'll both be grounded for life, but Little O will be flying free through his rainforest. I can live with that." I grinned, imagining flying on a vine with Little O.

Now to uncover my passport and a note from Dad. I twirled my hair totally frustrated. "THANKS for all the money, Matt! Team USA rocks! No clue how to find my passport and write the note but maybe the guys here will have an idea..."

CHAPTER 24

NIGHT EIGHT

After dinner, out at the swings, I told Zaqi and Bima about the amazing money collection from Matt. "Think he'll take $178?"

Bima's face instantly turned as tough as a gangster's—spitting out his words like gunshots. "That man," he said narrowing his eyes, "he will accept it, or we steal Little O."

"Guys, Matt is sending his money to Western Union and we can pick it up there. Well, I hope so. He says I need a letter from my dad and my passport and I don't have either."

No one said anything for a while and then Bima spoke up. "You need note from your dad. You write?" he asked.

"Me write?" I replied. To cover my nerves, I grinned. He wanted me to forge a letter? Next crime counterfeiting? The trip to jail got shorter every day. "I guess?"

"You find passport?" Bima's serious face meant business.

"I will check his desk if I can sneak in there sometime." So, forgery and stealing: check. My smile wobbled. "So, here's the full checklist: we need to buy Little O from Maniac Man, get to Gunung Leuser, but we don't know how to get there, and we must pick the day!" Then, I stalled out. If everything worked, Little O lived forever in the rainforest and I'd never see him again.

To stop the knot from forming in my stomach, I kicked up high. What if something bad happened to Little O while transporting him? We were taking total control of Little O's life, a baby, an orphan, my friend and he had no say in it. Like I had no say when my dad moved us here. Was I doing the right thing? Was there a better way?

"Hey, you okay? You not look so good." Bima smiled at me. "Zaqi name you Wani. You very brave."

Searching deep inside for Wani, who had disappeared even though I need her to stay. This rescue required full-on Wani, both feet in. First, get Little O there and then, he'd be safe with his mother.

Meanwhile, Zaqi's face melted further into misery. Lately, he lived on The Blues Train. "We go back to house. Google a map to Gunung Leuser rainforest?"

Walking home, my other worry crushed my mood. How could we find his mother in a giant rainforest? Could babies sniff out their mothers? Would she know he was there? Then I remembered that I hadn't told the guys about my last dream.

"Guys let me tell you about the dream I had a couple of nights ago when I met up with the auntie again. Wish it was his mom, so we'd know how to find her. Maybe she'll come to my next dream!"

Both Bima and Zaqi were impressed that I kept having orangutan dreams, but neither one had any ideas about how to find the mom. And none of us understood what the gun shots meant. Seemed like that was the thing we kept dodging. No one wanted to face the fact that we might not be able to find her there, which to me was the biggest missing piece.

Back at the house, on the computer, it didn't take long to find the road we'd need to drive.

"Look, only 80 kilometers," Zaqi said. "But say road bad in some spots. Dangerous with my bad scooter driving." Zaqi plopped his head in his hand rolling his eyes around.

Bima smacked him on the back. "Tough up! You do this. Little O be free!"

"Let's Skype Matt and tell him we're all set and to wire the money Thursday. Hey, should I handwrite or print the note from my dad on the computer?"

"You write like Dad?" Zaqi stared at me shaking his head. "How do?"

"Well, I used to forge his name sometimes at home back in Seattle. If I'd forget to get his signature on a permission slip or an assignment," I chortled. "And no one ever caught me, but I've never written a whole letter. I think I can though..."

Zaqi's eyes opened wide. "You forge father name? Not good. Too many wrong things. I say no."

"But Zaqi, what else can I do?" I said.

Bima grinned approvingly at me, his accomplice in crime, but Zaqi got up and walked out of the room. Mad and disappointed with me again and maybe ready to quit.

"Here, let me give it a shot." I picked up a pen and began to write. "My life of crime begins. Nothing boring about living in Sumatra, that's for sure."

Writing the note was tougher than I thought. I tore up the first one and then, scrapped the second one because it looked like kid-writing not man-writing. Finally, on the third try, I got it close enough and showed it to Bima, who nodded his approval.

Later, I mulled over the consequences of my latest crime. What would Dad say if he caught me? So many hurdles to accomplish our mission. How to get past Maniac Man and the scary scooter ride to Gunung Leuser. But the most important thing, my responsibility to keep Little O safe, to protect him with my life. Forgery, lying, that was nothing. But the escape put a baby orangutan's life on the line.

I took out my phone to look at photos of Little O. There he was, adorable, innocent and loving, and he trusted me. We were coming to save him. Soon, he'd be free in the rainforest.

CHAPTER 25

NIGHT EIGHT CONTINUES

On my way upstairs, Dad called me into the computer room.

"Jaylynn, I need to know exactly why you were writing my name on scraps of paper but not in your handwriting? Exactly what are you up to?" His face went all German Shepherd, his eyes burrowing into me demanding the truth. Anger filled all the cracks.

Pressure on, I had to come up with something fast, without showing signs of lying. Quite the challenge for someone breaking into being a juvenile delinquent. No panting, no sweaty palms, no tears or the whole mission would be ruined. But what lie could I tell? And how would I keep my voice normal when I was scared to death of being caught. A series of possibilities floated past but none of them were any good. Why would a girl write her dad's signature in his handwriting? Casual, I had to make it casual and hope he hadn't searched the rest of the scraps of the note. The silence between us was deafening.

"That? It's nothing. Just a little challenge I gave myself to write in someone else's style. I saw this YouTube video about this guy who could write anyone's signature in their handwriting like someone who can imitate voices. But I'm not any good at it." I smiled and rolled my eyes all innocent and dumb looking, I hoped.

Dad remained quiet intensifying my fear. Not now. We're so close. Please don't let him catch us now. My smile was painted on, my breathing rapid. Guilt was painted all over my face as the guillotine readied to drop.

"I see," Dad said. He gave me the kind of stare designed to break me down but Wani appeared—tough, daring. "Maybe try different challenges than my signature from now on. Good night, Jaylynn."

To be on the safe side, I gave him a hug. It felt bittersweet to be such a good liar. Tricking my dad was not something I wanted to be good at, but Little O's freedom hung in the balance.

Back in my room, I flopped belly first onto my mattress, recovering from a really close call, both happy and disappointed in myself. I pounded my frustrations onto my pillow. *POW!* Lying to Dad. *WHOMP!* Buy Little O. *BAM!* Steal Little O. *UMPF!* Find his mom. *WHAM!* Maybe if I hit harder, things would go the right way. I pounded so hard that I slipped off my bed and whispered, "Me, Wani, I need help to make the right choices." I put my head on the edge of the bed, listening, waiting, but no one sent any answers.

By the time Dad knocked on my door, I was back under the covers, all hunkered down and pretending to be asleep. He kissed me on my forehead and I felt his gentle hands tousle my hair and move the blanket over my shoulders. Not a great feeling, being deceitful, hiding the Great Rescue from him. I dreaded what would happen if he caught me and my mighty team: Zaqi, Bima, and Matt. I drifted off with one thought. We needed to get this done—soon!

CHAPTER 26

NIGHT EIGHT ENDS

When I opened my eyes, my face rested on an orangutan chest, her arms surrounding me. I sighed. This place was the safest place on earth. Her arms held me close, my breathing synced with hers. Gazing around, only green surrounded me on this treetop. The breeze gently blew across my face. Green in a million different shades, the sunshine lighting the leaves from above, light filtering through the branches. Breathing deeply, the moist, earthy smells of my home here. No wonder Little O used green so much. Green was more than a color here. It was a feeling, no, more than that—it was life. A moment I hoped lasted forever.

Feeling yellow all around me as well, I smiled.

"Little one, you are awake. You have had a good long sleep, safe in my arms."

"Yes, thank you. And now can you help me find Little O's mother? I want to bring him back here to live with her. I haven't worked it out yet, but we have a scooter. Can you take me to her?"

"I thought you knew."

"Knew what?"

"Your mother was shot. She is dead now."

"My... my... my mother?" My voice wavered as my stomach turned. I didn't know how that could be unless, unless... "You must think I am Little O, Auntie. No, no, I am Jaylynn."

"Ah Little O. Let me wrap you up in my arms. You have forgotten what happened on that terrible day." She told me the story of how 'my' mother was shot, killed by a man trying to steal me.

"Your mother tried hard to protect you, hiding in the leaves, climbing away, but the man shot her. She dropped to the earth. Dead. You were frightened, clutching her dead body and the man ripped you from her and stole you away. She is dead sweet Little O."

"NO! NO! THAT CAN'T BE!" I screamed. Turning to talk to her, I awoke on my floor, cringing, my chest rising and falling, my hands shielding my eyes. His mom can't be dead. Tears gushed out and I covered my head with my arms. That can't be right. Had to be a nightmare. Not even close to true. Before I could get my thoughts in order, I passed out in a lump on the floor.

CHAPTER 27

DAY NINE

With the countdown for the rescue headed downhill, I thought maybe I'd take a walk to the market after school for a Little O visit. Instead, the dream weighed heavy and was beyond depressing. Dead. Little O had no mother. My quest to rescue Little O was sacked. Ruined. Wrecked. No reason to take him to the rainforest now. Now to break the bad news about my dream to Zaqi, Bima, and Matt. Why drive Little O to Gunung Leuser?

Before breakfast, frustrated to the max, unable to accept the end of Little O's journey to freedom, I rushed to the computer to google 'shoot mother orangutan' figuring that nothing would come up. Instead all kinds of dreadful facts came up, even photos. Panic from my nightmare paralyzed me.

"The trade in baby orangutans — though illegal — continues to thrive. Hundreds of infant orangutans are taken from the wild for the pet trade every year. This trade is done by killing the mother and taking the baby."

I scrolled down and read out loud.

My heart beat in my throat. The blood drained from my face. Those dreadful words echoed in my mind and turned my stomach inside out. Maniac Man had shot her and stolen Little O.

"NO, it can't be. NO!" I protested. "Please say that's not true. Someone shot his mother and he saw it happen? Then they stole him? To sell him?" I shrieked, throwing my arms up into the air. Tears streamed down my cheeks. "HORRIBLE PEOPLE!"

In silence, reviewing everything. Like all my other dreams, my nightmare was true. Fact: Little O's mother was shot dead. Fact: My quest to return Little O to the rainforest had been broken up. Fact: There could be no mission. My head hit the desk as reality banged away at my heart. Even Wani couldn't stop the tears.

Zaqi walked in and immediately asked, "What wrong? Why cry?"

Trying to catch my breath, I pointed to the screen.

His eyebrows furrowed as he kept reading and then turned his gaze to me. A big thick fog covered his face. "It bad."

"It's over. We don't have a way to save him now. No mother."

We looked at each other with the same alarm.

"But maybe not true. Maybe Little O mother still alive. You not know true."

Biting my lower lip still hesitant to tell him about my nightmare. "How can we get Little O back to the rainforest if his mom isn't there? Who'll take care of him? We can't drop him off at a daycare. How can he survive?" I asked. My fingers gripped the mouse tightly telling myself not to throw it at the screen. "All of a sudden, all of this is too much. My head's whirling. I mean, I figured we'd find a way to get Little O back to his mom. Now I'm not positive he has a mom. Things got complicated," I cried. "We have to figure it out. But how?" My mouth opened, but no words appeared as sadness clouded my heart. So, now what? Could we let Little O live his life starving at the end of the chain?

Zaqi stared at the screen and cleared his throat. "Um," he began, "*Ibu* say always answer for problem. We find. Maybe Mother not shot dead. Maybe we find. Keep easy," he said slowly, glancing at me.

Still chewing on my lip, I mumbled, "I still don't understand: why shoot any mother to steal her baby and then sell him? That's cruel."

We both sat quietly, stumped.

Then, from somewhere deep inside, a faint voice told me to stop fretting and to stop crying. Little O needed me now. Little O needed action! Lifting my head, spurred on by this new inner strength, remembering Little O's trust in me. True, I'd never thought of myself as either brave or strong, but maybe I'd sold myself short. Looking straight at Zaqi, and pronouncing my words slowly and carefully, surprising myself with my own resolve, I said, "I've never saved anything, not even an injured bird, but I'll save Little O."

Zaqi looked straight into my eyes and smiled. "You stop cry? You strong," he said. "I help. We save Little O," he replied.

At that moment, Dad walked in. "My goodness, what

has you both tied up? Are you crying Jaylynn? You look too miserable to head off to school. Are you ill?"

"We're researching orangutans trying to find out all about them. Some of this stuff makes me miserable, sad, angry, too," I muttered. My eyes focused on Dad waiting for his reaction.

"Honey, I'm sorry. Gita has breakfast ready. Let's go eat something delicious and you both can tell us what you've been reading."

Sitting down at the table, Dad let a smile steal across his face. "So, Jaylynn and Zaqi, let's hear what you perused on the internet."

No other way, but to spit it out. I said, "We read a horrifying thing."

"Horrifying? Tell me," he sighed.

"Well, well, we read that they shoot the mothers in order to steal the babies and then sell them." When I glanced at Zaqi, a frown crept across his face stealing the light. "That means that Little O's mom may be dead and maybe that man shot her and that's why he's selling Little O. How can they allow the killing of mother orangutans?"

Dad cleared his throat, a sure sign that The Speech had arrived. "Ah, Jaylynn, life everywhere including the rainforest contains struggles and hardship." His eyebrows raised as he eyed me closely. "There's little that can be done to change things."

Gita glanced at Dad and then at me. "Jaylynn, I sad, very sad. It true?" Gita asked softly.

"*Ya, Ibu.* We want big work save Little O," Zaqi said.

Words burst out of my mouth. "How can that happen?

Isn't it illegal?" I asked. My voice stronger, I kept the tears at bay and my temper from boiling over. "What about Little O's mother?"

Gita rubbed her arms as if standing outside in the cold. "*Madu*, no legal this thing. Bad thing. Maybe need money for family. Maybe bad man. Not know which."

"So, a man needs money and he shoots an orangutan." Muttering silent swear words to myself, twirling my hair around my finger, trying to understand. "I still don't get it." Though my insides churned, I commanded myself to stay strong.

Zaqi folded his arms across his chest. "*Ibu*, that terrible. Why kill orangutan so beautiful?"

"Let me chime in," Dad said rubbing his chin with his hand. "It's all about money, economics. Sometimes, when people all over the world need to make money, they're in direct conflict with laws or with protecting their natural resources. It's a constant battle. Money drives the world, not long-range planning to protect the environment. The problem you discuss holds many more complications than I'm explaining, but can you begin to understand?"

We remained silent, stunned into stillness. Zaqi clenched his fists under the table. My inner teapot steamed, pressure building, ready to pop. Patience remained one of my areas of weakness. Mom used to tell me to breathe or count to ten or take a walk to keep from getting exasperated and losing my temper. Dad showed no compassion for Little O and zero understanding for me. I counted to ten.

"I'm proud of you both for digging in and asking questions. Keep looking. Maybe find out which conservation groups work to protect orangutans and you can join them, but a rescue is out of the question for Little O."

"We'll keep researching, but Zaqi and I want to concentrate on saving one baby orangutan. It might be difficult, close to impossible, but it's one really important thing."

CHAPTER 28

DAY NINE
CONTINUES

After that conversation, studying was the last thing on my mind. The Great Orangutan Rescue took all my concentration. Every part of the plan hinged on his mother, who was probably dead. If not, there was only a slim chance we'd discover her in the wild. Gita's voice played over and over in my head. We must believe we could do this. Little O deserved life in the rainforest.

Slouched back in my seat, sighing my millionth sigh, I headed to my room, plopped on my bed and stared at the ceiling fan, perplexed. But I 'heard' Little O and Auntie and talked to them too. Why could we talk to each other? Was my dad right or was Gita and I simply needed to believe? Then, an idea hit me. I ran to the computer to Google 'rescue baby orangutans Indonesia' like, maybe Wikipedia had a plan we could use. Bingo! There it was.

"Batu Mbelin is the only quarantine and care centre for the Sumatran orangutan."

But what did that mean? Quarantine sounded bad. I kept reading.

"Illegally held orangutans that are confiscated in Sumatra are taken to the Batu Mbelin Care Centre. Many have been kept as pets or have been injured by palm oil plantation workers. Orangutans are given a full medical check upon arrival and treated for any illnesses and parasites. They undergo a quarantine period before being introduced to other compatible orangutans. Many confiscated orangutans are very young and require regular milk feeds. Young orangutans have full time carers during the day and night and are also given tree climbing lessons in the grounds."

The Care Centre was a nursery for orphans? With full time caretakers? Learning to climb trees in a forest school? But what happened to them when they grew up? I didn't want him living in some cage for his whole life.

"When orangutans are deemed suitable for release they are either sent to the Bukit Tigapuluh release center in the province of Jambi or to the Jantho Reintroduction Centre in the province of Aceh. As of the end of 2010, over 220 orangutans had been received at the Batu Mbelin Care Centre, with 135 orangutans transferred to Jambi for release and six transferred to the newly established Jantho Reintroduction Centre. Over 120 Sumatran orangutans from Batu Mbelin have been released into the wild since the first release in 2003."

I couldn't believe it, 120 baby orphans released into the rainforest, as in free? Little O would be taught to survive and then released into the rainforest? No more heavy chain, no more sitting in the dirt, alone, scared, hungry. No more beatings from Maniac Man. This place sounded like a perfect solution. Would Bima and Zaqi agree?

"The Batu Mbelin Care Centre is located near Medan in North Sumatra."

Near Medan? No way! Close to us? But there was one huge downside. If we took him there, he'd never see his mom again. Ever. As his friend, could I make that decision? I knew how much I missed my mom, but my dreams said she was dead and so did the internet. His mom was dead. He was now an orphan.

After dinner, Zaqi and I walked out to the swings to meet Bima.

Zaqi smiled his biggest grin ever. "Drive scooter not easy, but I better now. Bima say we drive every day till we drive to rainforest. We keep secret from *Ibu.*"

"And Dad," I croaked.

"Two days maybe three, I ready drive. But I not know way. Let's check out the map on the computer. Gunung Leuser Rainforest here we come!" He paused.

"What wrong? Hair twirl mean unhappy."

"Well, two or three days would make it the weekend.

Can you be ready for Friday? But our big problem is finding his mother. I'm sure she is dead. How can we find her in the rainforest Zaqi?"

Zaqi's face scrunched up.

"I researched this site, Batu Mbelin, a rescue center for orphan orangutans. I want you to look at it. Little O will like it there and be returned to the rainforest."

"What?" All that happiness drained right out of his face. He kicked his legs into the dirt, stopped swinging. "Jaylynn, I…I…no get. Not go Gunung Leuser? No mom?" Zaqi grimaced and without saying a word, let me know his reaction to this new idea.

"I know, but…but… what if his mom can't be found? Remember what we read. And my dream." I got quiet. "I'm sorry," I whispered.

We both drew back on our swings, and kicked out our legs, flying as high as the swings allowed. The creak of metal the only sound.

I skidded to a stop and watched Zaqi, who looked off in distance focusing on something far away. His face forlorn, no joy, no words, no smile, and no friend. *Roadblock.* I knew how mad I'd made him, and kicked hard taking the swing up again, but nothing changed, no matter how hard and high I swung. I glanced at him hoping his anger had melted but he wouldn't even look at me. Skidding to a stop, I walked back to the house alone, feeling like I'd failed my best friend in Sumatra.

Back on the computer, the Skype bell rang. Matt. Thank goodness!

"Everyone wants to help save a baby orangutan.

Someone's even starting an orangutan club. I'll be ready to send it all this afternoon."

"Right. Zaqi's still practicing driving his cousin's scooter, but he said it's getting easier."

"So, what's wrong? You're pouting."

"Sorry. Zaqi's angry at me and stopped talking." I sighed. "Let me tell you about my dream."

Matt listened intently. "That's a crazy dream."

"It gets worse. I found that it's true on the internet. Our original plan is over. Totally over!"

"Take it easy. So, what about Zaqi? Why's he mad?"

"I Googled a rescue center and found one where they teach orphan orangutans to live in the wild and then release them into the rainforest. That's got to be better for Little O. He can't live without a mother in Gunung Leuser, end of story."

"But that place is a huge switcheroo. So, Zaqi doesn't like it?" How about Bima?"

"Zaqi's officially not talking to me. He probably won't even help now. Bima doesn't know about it yet."

"Send the link. We want what's best for Little O. Going to the rescue center means he never ever ever sees his mom again. Right?""Hmm….yeah. I hate that part of the rescue center. But she's dead. I'm sure."

"What the heck? Wani, you're saving Little O. Wish I was there with you." Matt looked at me, his eyes wishful, and then he sighed, shoulders sagging.

"How cool if you flew here to join The Great Orangutan Rescue. Will your parents let you come visit?"

"Ha, fat chance of that. They barely let me ride the bus

downtown. But at least I can help from here, right? Talk soon. I'll send the money to Western Union after school today. And then the next day The Great Orangutan Rescue scores! Remember your name, Wani, which means daring."

I twirled my hair faster. "You think? Dude, I don't know."

Matt gave his go-to answer. "No time for doubts. Sleep on it."

"Yeah, you're right. I gotta bounce." I said good bye and thought about the rescue center.

After all, I was adjusting to life without a mom. Maybe Little O could adjust, too. I gawked at my reflection in the computer screen searching for Wani, who must have been hiding. My audacious self had to be in there somewhere. The countdown was at two.

CHAPTER 29

NIGHT NINE

That night Matt surprised me after supper with a call back. "I've been thinking a lot about the plan."

"You look at that rescue center?"

"Yeah. It looks cool and really good for babies. I want to go there, too and help teach babies to live in the rainforest. Is it a long drive from where you are?"

"No, closer than the rainforest."

"But still, the rainforest has his mom.... maybe..." Matt said.

"What if we ride Little O to the rainforest and can't find his mom? Then what?"

"Tough choice. No mom ever at the rescue center," Matt said.

"But I've never dreamt about his mom. Think about that. Only Auntie."

Matt scratched his cheek then covered his mouth. "How long to drive to both? Long enough for your dad to probably go nuts after he figures out, you're gone?"

"Whatever," I said. The whole plan was aggravating. Too gnarly. Every part of the old plan hinged on returning him to his mother. Failure was knocking on my door and Zaqi was mad. The rescue was a swamp filling with alligators and poisonous snakes.

"If no Zaqi, no one drives. I can't do this by myself. I'm going to bed. Good night."

Flopping myself, belly first onto my bed, I gave Little O's mom a plea. "I'm going to sleep now. I want you in my dreams and I want you to tell me if you're dead or alive. Mom or no mom?"

I pounded my pillow. *POW!* Mom. *BAM!* No mom. *UMPF!* Rescue Center. *WHAM!* Rainforest. All the things that I didn't understand. My head hit the pillow ready for sleep but then I remembered... my passport.

Waiting for the cover of darkness, sounds of night filled my ears as Dad's snoring drifted to my room, and my next crime began. Sneaking down the hall, past Dad's bedroom, tiptoeing down the stairs to his office and walking into the darkened room, my toe banged into an unseen end table forcing me to slap my hand over my mouth to muffle my moan. Still as a statue, I waited. No one. As my eyes adjusted to the darkness, Dad's desk rose out of the dark like a mountain ready for an expedition. Slowly pulling out each drawer, rustling through papers like a thief, searching for the feel of that little blue book, my passport.

Mom always said search as if you know you can capture. Time for a closer examination but then footsteps in the hall startled me. Crouching down low, hidden behind the desk, I waited. If caught, no number of lies could conceal the truth. Someone walked past the office. Gita? Zaqi? Dad? Returning, they stood in the doorway breathing. Had they heard me? Not a muscle on my body twitched as I held my breath. Waiting. Finally, whoever it was moved away.

What if they came back? Working in the dark, rifling through each drawer again, figuring that Dad would stash it towards the back of a drawer, in a binder. I pulled out the top drawer, reaching to the back. Moving my fingers around, pens, tape, stapler and then, a small packet. YES! Both of our passports! I snatched mine, closed the drawer and hoped no one waited to trap me out in the hall.

Tiptoeing towards the stairs, making a smooth getaway, until fingers on my shoulder made me gasp. Immobile, stock-still, frozen stiff, clutching my passport to my chest. Hooked. Captured. Apprehended. Grounded forever.

"Jaylynn?" Gita whispered.

Turning slowing, moving the passport behind my back. I gave Gita a half-sick grin.

"I… I… needed a memory stick," I squeaked.

"*Ya.*"

"…for school."

"Missy Jaylynn, you work hard school. Not easy, *ya?*" Her gentle grin. Her eyes warm with caring. When she hugged me, my head dropped in shame.

But she put her hand under my chin and raised my face. Looking straight into my eyes, she said, "New life here give you challenge, *ya?*"

All I could do was hug Gita. Not about to lie to my fairy godmother. Caught but not punished. With relief, I sailed up the stairs, with one last thought, Little O's mom, please be in my dream tonight if you're still alive.

CHAPTER 30

DAY TEN

Morning brought a burst of energy and nerves. Freedom Day minus one. Today we'd ride to Western Union, pick up the money, take a practice drive and be all set for tomorrow.

At breakfast, I crunched Cheerios in a giant bowl with bananas, and cold milk. "Thanks for getting cereal. It's freaking awesome. Like home."

Gita's eyes lit up and she smiled her heart smile, flooding my system with guilt for getting Zaqi all tangled up saving Little O.

"*Sayang*, I like it, too!" Gita said.

"Not me," Zaqi said. He made a face full of disdain and turned up his nose. "Cold milk? Not taste good. Cheerios? They like paper. Not spicy. Not sweet. Too cold. *Nasi Goreng* good for me."

Finished with my cereal, I poked Zaqi to hurry up, but his face told me to lay off. When we headed to school, my voice heavy with dread, I spit out my words. "So, I need your help." I sighed. "That baby orangutan rescue center about an hour outside of Medan? Will you look at it again?

Maybe Little O should go there?"

"What? Not understand. Not rainforest?" Zaqi asked. His face turned sour.

"We have to choose what's best for him." I stopped talking when I saw the look on his face, hesitating, not wanting to dig a deeper pit, but then I spit it out at machine gun speed, hating what I had to say. "We can't transport him to Gunung Leuser. Breaks my heart but his mom is dead. We can't leave him there with no one to protect him. And then, if she's alive by some miracle, well, how do we find her in a giant rainforest? Can we wander around with him and hope we find her? She never comes to my dreams. Do you know absolutely his mom is alive? I'm totally in if you do."

"I quit. Not help. Little O need mother." Without even looking at me, he ran up the schoolyard steps, two at a time, slammed his hands on the front doors shoving them open, exactly like last time. Mad at me again.

All of my fears about the Great Rescue returned. He wouldn't help me get Little O to Batu Mbelin. Worse, he wouldn't be my friend anymore either. Now it was up to Bima to help Little O and I wasn't sure he'd do it …for the same reason. It just didn't feel right to leave Zaqi out of it. The rescue was headed for disaster. And what if Little O's mom really was alive?

After school on the walk home, I waved but Zaqi ignored me and walked ahead. If he refused to talk to me, I'd never be able to pull off the rescue. Counting the lines on the sidewalk and trying to figure out if I could rescue Little O without him, absorbed in thought, the sound of Bima's voice shocked me.

"You scared me!"

"Zaqi and you not walk together? What's going on?" he demanded.

"Zaqi's angry at me because I told him that we have to drive Little O to Batu Mbelin, the rescue center. It's better there. He'll learn how to survive before finally being released in the wild. But Zaqi wants us to go to the Gunung Leuser, the place Auntie told me about in my dream. He wants Little O to grow up with his mom." As I spoke, my stomach contracted as if wrung out by giant hands. Clenching my fists, bracing myself for another fuming boy, I turned my head and narrowed my eyes threateningly at Bima. "It's not smart driving Little O to Gunung Leuser, with no way to find his mother, who I am sure is dead." That last bit flattened out my resolve. Every time I thought about Little O's mom, I traded determination for indecision.

Bima nodded and said, "*Ya*. You make good choice. Poor Little O. They shoot mother. Steal him. The Gunung Leuser Rainforest not good for Little O. No mother there."

A weight lifted off my shoulders with Bima's support. Would Bima help me even if Zaqi wouldn't. "Smart? Is that what you think? Awesome!" My tight fists loosened. Bima was the best.

"I talk to Zaqi."

Bima ran up ahead, but as we walked into the house, Zaqi still wasn't talking to me. Gita smiled at us, but for certain, she could tell something was wrong. She talked to Bima in Bahasa. I recognized *skuter* because it sounded exactly like English. My eyes darted nervously back and forth between Bima and Zaqi. Had Gita figured it out?

Feeling too much tension, I escaped to my room, plunked onto my bed and grabbed my headphones, singing my heart out, and gazing up at the ceiling, trying to figure out how to get Little O to the sanctuary without help from Zaqi and without the grownups discovering my plot. Focus on the goal. No matter what, Little O ends up in the rainforest. We're coming for you, baby, and your life will turn green, yellow, and free.

Getting up, I settled in front of the computer to figure out how to get to Batu Mbelin Care Centre using Google Maps. Trouble was without those guys I had no clue about the map. Bima walked in, smiling.

"Right now, I'm trying to figure out the map to the center. Want to look at it?"

"Whole map, even what streets to turn on." Bima leaned in, tensing his fingers around the mouse. "I not know this location." His voice grew quiet, almost a whisper. "But 30 minutes away? Close. Zaqi say not go."

"If Zaqi say no, rescue is over. No one can drive," I said.

Our heads bent towards the computer and I looked at Bima, who shifted his face into a smile.

"You pull off The Great Rescue in one day? *Ya?*"

"Not without your help!" I covered up my nerves with a double dose of fake enthusiasm.

Zaqi walked in and his face still plastered with anger. "I no drive there. No mother there. Bad for Little O." Zaqi crossed his arms, glaring at me.

"So, you navigate, I drive," Bima said completely ignoring his cousin.

I automatically rubbed my leg, remembering my last

165

ride on the scooter and the crash. Truth be told, that scooter gave me the jitters every time I got on. Now I'd hold Little O, while telling Bima where to turn and stay on the scooter.

"I not drive," Zaqi repeated.

"*Ya*, north on *Jalan Glugur*, then second left onto *Jl. Jend Gatot Subroto*, then left onto *Jl. Iskandar Muda* and then…" Bima said still ignoring Zaqi.

"Hold it. Hold it right there. Houston, we have a problem," I grumbled.

"Houston? What means Houston?" Bima asked me.

"The space shuttle… a movie… never mind." I scrunched up my eyes not wanting to show any fear. "You guys know that I can't read these street signs. Right? It's like an endless maze. I'll try really hard, but I don't know," I murmured.

Bima studied me. I quickly tucked my hands under the desk to hide my clenched fists and he raised an eyebrow.

"Maybe we practice run part of way? Now. Okay?" he decreed.

"But we have to pick up the money from Western Union too, right?" I wound a strand of hair around my finger repeatedly and pushed down the pressure that kept building up. Zaqi's face tangled into sadness but he wasn't talking. Maybe his sadness was about Little O's mom or maybe about lying to his own mom, but his face flooded with the blues. He caught me staring at him and blew out fast like a whale.

"We go Western Union. Then practice drive. Now." Bima said.

"I not go." Zaqi turned and left the room. My best friend in Sumatra walked out.

CHAPTER 31

DAY TEN
CONTINUES

As I entered the Western Union door, I cleared my throat. "Hello. I believe a money wire has arrived for me. Jaylynn O'Reilly."

The shrewd bank teller scrutinized me, but not a word left his thin-lipped mouth. He stood at attention, barely moving.

I fought the urge to stick out my tongue. I marched to the counter, meeting him eyeball to eyeball. "From Matt Bernard, in the amount of $76 US, which converts to 1,069,334 Rupiah."

Again, silence. Sharp missiles shot out of his eyes, obviously experienced at breaking juvenile delinquents. He crossed his arms.

"Sir?" I remembered that wild animals can smell fear in their prey. Tilting his head, he looked at me out of the corner of his eyes, his maximum criminal probe. He examined me for a good long time, but I stayed strong.

"Here's my passport."

The man pushed his thick black glasses back on his nose and began to write down all my information. Then he turned to get something from the back desk. I held my posture. When he opened the cash drawer, I silently screamed, *YES!* Slowly, he counted out 962,401 Rupiah and stopped.

"There is a 107,000 Rupiah charge to receive this money." And then he smacked his hand hard on top of the money, startling me. He peered straight into my eyes.

"You have permission from your parents?" he grumbled. He kept one hand on my passport and the other on the money.

Only my eyes moved as I tried to calculate how much he had charged me. So, one dollar is like 13,000 Rupiah. I needed to make a proportion. 1:13000 = x: 116000. Too much math. From somewhere deep inside, my well of courage asked him, "Sir, please, tell me in dollars how much you charged me?"

"I charged $8.90, one percent."

Reaching into my backpack, I pulled out the envelope with Dad's, well, my letter. When I started to chew my lower lip, I caught myself and stopped. The man read the letter slowly, pursing his lips, occasionally glancing up into my eyes.

"Okay, here is your passport and here is the money."

Leaving the store, somehow keeping myself from jumping up and cheering, when I saw Bima, I flashed a thumbs up. "Let's get out of here fast. I have the money!" I grinned, proud of my newly established strength. I loved this moment. No way would I ever forget it.

"Good work. Hop on! Time for practice on the first five turns to Batu Mbelin so we be ready for the real thing tomorrow."

With all the traffic and lack of street signs, we missed the first turn and had to turn around. I held on to Bima with one arm and pretended to hold Little O with the other, protecting him. When the next turn came up too fast, we missed it and had to turn around again. We made the third turn but missed the next two. By the time we slogged our way through all five turns, less than half way to the center, we were totally discouraged. Our practice had taught us how tough the drive would be and how much we missed Zaqi. It had taken hours and we still had over half of the trip left to travel.

"I get you home now. It late."

Arriving home, Bima shouted at Zaqi, "Let's go to the swings."

At the swings, no one listened to anyone else. All three of us shouted out at the same time, the boys in Bahasa, me in English, a cacophony of shouts getting louder all the time.

"I not drive. Not go to rescue center. Little O needs mother."

"I'm not positive I can hold onto Bima while holding Little O and not fall off."

"I concentrate on driving."

"*Ibu* know what I do."

"What if Little O won't sit with me on the scooter?"

"*SEMUA ORANG BERHENTI BICARA!*" Bima yelled.

I recognized those words from school. Quiet! I looked at the boys with their dead serious faces and thought about all our shouting. Choking off a laugh, I tried to control myself. I cupped my hand over my mouth, not wanting to make them mad, but a laugh snuck out. They grew silent, looking at me, not pleased with my laughter.

At first, Bima frowned at me, exasperated, I guess, to hear me laugh, but then his eyes twinkled, his smile appeared, and he started laughing, too. Zaqi shook his head at the two of us, and for the first time smiled.

Back and forth our swings flew, and my face beamed up at the endless blue cloudless sky that stretched above us.

"Jaylynn, you like super hero now?" Bima's grin looked more like a smirk.

Happy to be teased, but I didn't want to show it. When I reached over and smacked him on the side of the head, Zaqi snorted.

"Well, we're on track, you guys. You should come back, Zaqi. I need you. So does Little O." I perked up my chin and sat taller in the swing. The courage inside was here to stay.

"*Ya*. I want him free but not sanctuary. No mother," Zaqi said.

Bima watched us and said, "I drive tomorrow."

Staring at his cousin, Zaqi pursed his lips, speechless. A sigh escaped his lips and he turned to me. My eyes hit the ground not wanting to make him angry. I blew air through my lips like a horse and pumped harder, flew higher.

Then Zaqi shouted out, "I NOT GO!"

Bima jerked his head around, paused one cool second. "*Ya*, okay. But *Sepupu*, need you."

"You have to come Zaqi. Little O loves you. We'll ditch school and save Little O!" I said. Pumping my swing hard, thankful to have Bima but not yet Zaqi.

"School call home when absent." Zaqi asked.

"Ya, school call my house but *Ibu* work. And Gita?"

Zaqi's voice grew quiet, almost a whisper. "She home all day. She answer phone. She learn we not there. Worry."

The image of Gita's face at breakfast haunted me. Her disappointment. And there it was. Our biggest obstacle, lying to Gita, betraying her trust. Gita would discover we weren't in school and would figure out that we were rescuing the baby orangutan, but she wouldn't know where or how, and didn't that mean she'd have to tell Dad?

Not even Bima could figure out how to solve that worry. We all loved her. Bima broke the silence. "We must work fast. First market, buy Little O. Or steal. Then ride fast to Batu Mbelin. Make all turns. Come right back. Fast."

"Right. Fast," I said. Picturing Maniac Man yelling at Little O, hitting him and then of course, when he grabbed me, I bit my lower lip, blinking fast. My stomach flip-flopped, but I reached in deep. *Stay with courage, Wani. Gold, radiate gold.*

Bima's expression changed to hard and angry and he leaned forward, spoke slowly and clearly to us, punctuating his words sharply. "We steal if man not say yes to buy," he told us. "That man not keep him. No! Never!"

"I mad this man sell baby," Zaqi said. "I angry this man hit baby. I angry he grab you. I protect baby orangutan and you. But no steal. I not steal."

Stalled. Flat tires on the plan. No Zaqi. Tomorrow we'd bust out Little O. The biggest thing in my life. Saving Little O... or not.

"We're going to do this. Get Little O back to the rainforest. I can't do anything without you both. Zaqi, I'm going to tell you my last dream. Zaqi listened, listened to what Auntie said but then he turned his back and walked away. He left the team.

Bima shrugged. "If no Zaqi, we two can do. He wrong." With that he turned on his heels and walked away.

CHAPTER 32

GREAT RESCUE DAY ELEVEN

Groggy from a restless night with no dreams, I dressed quickly, grabbed my backpack, smiled at the jingle of change from all the money inside and rushed out of my bedroom to breakfast.

I had a tough time settling down. Guilt crawled up my pant leg right to my heart. After all, I'd led the charge to save Little O. Zaqi had never disobeyed any rules. Head down, crunching Cheerios, out of the corner of my eye, I spied a change. The big warm smile that lived on Gita's face was missing.

Checking out Dad, he seemed happy and calm almost like the pebble in his shoe had worked its way out. Generally oblivious to people's emotions, he surprised me when he noticed that Gita wasn't smiling. He sat up a little straighter, interested. "You feeling all right?"

Everything stopped, leaving my spoon in midair. She knew. I was certain. It stops here, the whole rescue over, permanently grounded. I caught Zaqi's eyes, and he replied with a minute shoulder shrug.

Gita looked at us and I fidgeted in my chair. The

churning in my stomach caused me to lose interest in my Cheerios. The tension at the table was palpable, churning my stomach like a vice. Well, except for Dad, who still hadn't figured out that we were up to no good.

Finally, after what seemed like hours, Gita cleared her throat, pulling out words, as if each one caused her pain. Her thickly lashed eyes glanced at Zaqi and then at Dad. "Mr. John, you right. I no feel good today."

Across the table, Zaqi stiffened as Gita observed him, straight through to his secret. The expression on Gita's face killed me. Even worse for Zaqi.

"Well, easy does it today. Rest remains the best solution." He grinned again, a heartfelt one. He glanced at his watch. "Hey, kids, hurry up. Have a good day."

I nodded, unable to speak, my mouth gone dry. Hugging him like a traitor harboring a top-secret conspiracy. I wanted to shout out the truth. *We're going to transport Little O to the Batu Mbelin Care Centre today. We're ditching school, riding a scooter, maybe even stealing him, Dad.* The truth like an itch at the center of my back, where I couldn't reach but, instead, I lowered my eyes to say goodbye to Gita, hating that I had betrayed her trust.

When Zaqi pushed up from his chair, heat crept up his neck. He gulped in a long breath and held it. Hugging his mom, I watched him. His voice cracked as he hugged her and whispered, "*Harap anda merasa Ibu lebih baik. Aku mencintaimu.*"

"What did you tell your mom just now?" I muttered.

"'Hope you feel better, Mother. I love you.' *Ibu* know. Her face sad. I sad," he muttered. "I never lie to *Ibu*. I not like. Have big sadness for *Ibu*. I not take Little O away from mother forever."

"I want him up in a tree, in a nest, cuddling, safe, I do. But think about it. Both my dream and the internet point to his mom having been shot. If he goes to the sanctuary, they will teach him rainforest skills, to survive on his own and someday he will be a free orangutan swinging through the trees. If we love him, this is our only answer." Shaking off my guilt like a horse shaking away bothersome flies, lying seemed a small price to pay for Little O's freedom.

When we saw Bima at our secret meeting spot, his smile stretched across his face from ear to ear. He signaled with his clenched fist in the air and shouted, "We free Little O today. Hop on."

Raising my fist sky high, I shouted, "Let's do this thing, guys." I hopped on the back of the scooter, taking a big breath to calm my battered nerves.

With his head down, Zaqi walked away and I lost my best friend.

"Zaqi wrong. Sanctuary only choice. Little O must be free. Hop on."

Even with Bima driving, the ride to the market, filled with trucks rattling and horns honking, was as harrowing as ever. I sealed my eyes shut when a bus came too close. At a stop light, Bima squeezed us in between a scooter and a becak. A grizzled man with messy hair and crumpled clothes drove the motorcycle part of the becak. A mother cradling her child protectively sat in the side car. *Pretty soon I'd be cuddling Little O, keeping him safe, too.*

Arriving at the market, we parked the scooter. A flock of

butterflies fluttered inside my stomach as I watched Bima, strong and tough and sure of himself.

"Come here, Jaylynn. Give me all but $5. We'll need that for gas," he told me. "So, we have $178, right?" His face gave nothing away. No fear. No worries.

"I recounted last night, 2,197,260 Rupiah."

He took the giant stack of bills and coins and placed it all in his front pocket patting it twice. "I will go to man to buy Little O." Bima pulled out a tool from his pocket and handed it to me. "You stay hidden near door. If you hear bargain not working, you sneak out and break link on chain."

Grabbing the tool and putting it in my pocket, an icy shiver ran down my spine. We walked into the store, Bima with a strong gait. Hidden from view, I peeked out between boxes.

"*Salamat pagi.*" Bima's friendly tone hid his anger.

Maniac Man looked up at Bima and quickly flicked his eyes back to his paper.

"*Apa yang akan kalian suka?*" He stepped closer to the counter. "*Kami berada di sini pada bisnis. Keluarga kami bekerja untuk ingin membeli orangutan. Berapa banyak?*"

"Orangutan?" He eyed Bima suspiciously, slowly placing his hand on his chin. He hitched up his head. From the look on his face, I doubted that he believed Bima had any money.

"3,500,000 rupiah," he told him and went back to his paper.

What? I didn't believe what I'd just heard. Impossible! He had said $200 which was 2,700,000 Rupiah and now he wanted 800,000 Rupiah more. I bit my lower lip. What would Bima do?

Bima shook his head like an experienced negotiator. "1,700,000," he retorted.

The man jerked his head back on his spindly neck, laughing. I trembled when I saw his menacing face. His eyes fired bullets at Bima. But suddenly, his face changed. Like a gear clicked in his greedy brain. Maybe he'd noticed the wad of rupiah in Bima's front pocket. Deliberately, knowingly, he asked in Bahasa scratching his cheek. "I know you?"

"No. Not know."

"2,800,000 *jumlah akhir*." His tone hard and cold and final.

Bima held firm, shook his head no and growled, "1,800,000." His voice didn't even waver.

The man hooted. "2,600,000" He clasped and unclasped his fingers in front of his chest

"*Terlalu tinggi. Kami pergi.* Good bye." Bima turned to leave.

"2,500,000 *ijab*" Maniac Man shouted, lowering his price. Maybe he would sell Little O after all. "You not get cheap deal!" he yelled. "Baby orangutan sell for much money." Maniac Man pursed his lips together and whistled loudly.

Bima shook his head no. "2,000,000 *ijab*." And started to walk away. I knew he'd be happy not to pay this man for Little O. But when they were almost out of the store, the man shouted after them. "*Ya. Ya.* 2,000,000."

Bima walked back and counted out the money, slowly. After he tallied 2,000,000, he held out his hand expecting the key. But Maniac Man grabbed the money quickly, his thick fingers holding it tight. "You bring 200,000 Rupiah more, you want orangutan."

"Give me key or I call police," Bima threatened.

Hearing that, I tiptoed out but heard Maniac Man say, "You cannot prove you gave me money. They not believe boy."

After leaving the store, angrier than I'd ever seen him, Bima ran over to me but empty handed. He had no key. He ranted in rapid fire Bahasa making fists out of his hands as his body tensed.

"Forget about him. We still must save Little O. Bima, help me pry open the link," I said.

His face filled with rage. "Work fast! Pry off link before man comes." Bima looked at me. "I fight him if he try stop us! I'm oldest. My responsibility keep you safe."

Little O clambered up into my lap as soon as I sat next to him and a shower of yellow filled me up inside and out. He swung his arms around me as if I was his mother, making sweet sounds as we hugged, and a sweet enchantment slid over me. My heart spilled open with happiness as my fingers brushed his cheeks.

"Little O, how I love you. Soon you'll be free floating on vines in the rainforest. We're saving you today," I said softly. Well, I hoped the plan worked and today started his new life.

As the link slowly pried open, Bima's hands slipped and he cut his fingers. He looked at the cut for a split second before wiping blood on his pants. "Almost done. You pick him up and run to the scooter. I right behind you unless...."

"Right. Wish I had a blanket to cover him." *Come on. Come on.* "You can do it. You're almost there."

But the last bit held tight. Even Little O watched Bima. His sweet little eyes staring at Bima, as he worked on his chain, his freedom. Finally, the link twisted open enough to slip off the chain but at that exact moment, we heard Zaqi yell frantically. Zaqi was here?

"*PRIA! PRIA!* MAN. MAN."

"*JAYLYNN*, HE'S FREE. NOW GO! RUN!"

I held Little O fast to my chest. "But, what… about you… and Zaqi?"

"GO… NOW… RUN!"

Zaqi shot out his arms and legs to block Maniac Man, who puffed up like a great horned owl. Zaqi looked like a miniature Dachshund yipping at a Doberman Pinscher.

Little O wrapped his arms tightly around my body, his hands gripping my hair as I turned to run away. When Maniac Man saw me escaping with the orangutan, he pushed Zaqi away. In response, Zaqi planted a hard kick square on his shin and then ran like the devil. Maniac Man let out a dreadful scream, rubbing his shin as he danced around on one leg. But as soon as he remembered Little O, he forgot his shin. With a quick glimpse over my shoulder, I tripled my speed. Maniac Man was coming after me and Little O. When I ducked behind a stall, I hoped that I'd eluded him. Slowly I peeped through a crack and saw Maniac Man looking for me. But Zaqi lunged at Maniac Man knocking him to the ground. Then Bima ran towards Maniac Man, slid on his left hip driving his right leg up as if going after a ball. Definitely a sliding tackle, a yellow card kind of sliding tackle. *Make it dirty, Bima; bring this guy down.* The tackle worked. Maniac Man hit the ground hard landing flat on his back. In that split second, Bima sprang to his feet. Time for me to get moving.

Darting through the crowd, sheltering Little O in my arms, the people stared at us. Terrified that Maniac Man might catch up, I ran full speed and when I finally made it to our scooter, gasping for air, my heart pounded in my chest. "Little O, we're safe. You're not going back there ever!"

Clutching Little O close to my chest like a mother protecting her baby. Little O's fingers pulled on my hair, pulling my head back. He looked into my eyes. I remembered my first day in Sumatra, when I'd found him. I didn't have a clue about life in Indonesia, but I had found my strength because of him.

Little O tugged harder and sent me red. Waves of red. More fear. I shook myself back to my senses showering him with yellow. *Be brave, Jaylynn. He needs you now. Grab this moment, this time to be brave and protect Little O.* But where were the boys? Shouldn't they be here by now?

CHAPTER 33

GRAND FINALE DAY ELEVEN

Worried sick about the boys, the wait at the scooter seemed like a million forevers. Little O's shivers of red grew stronger. Why weren't they back yet? Little O grabbed my hair and climbed on my head. We were both such a mess. Covered in red. Quivering with each breath. Before I knew it, my breathing matched his. Panting. Calm left me. Searching for a yellow thought to protect us both like a blanket, I only got red. Drawing Little O to my chest, breathing slowly to calm down.

When Bima and Zaqi sprang out of the crowd, I bit my lip to stop from crying. "What happened? I saw the tackle. I've been so afraid."

Out of breath, Bima spoke first. "No time," he panted. "Hop on. We fly out of here. Not good if Maniac Man find us."

Bima revved up the scooter. The engine roared. Little O squealed and popped his lips. "Poppoppoppoppoppop" His fear filled me up with so much blue that I could only gasp.

"Little O… is… too… alarmed." I panted. I tried to calm myself, but my breath filled with all kinds of hitches.

"We can't make him ride." Little O's arms intertwined with mine.

"We have no choice. We can't stop now," Bima insisted. "Farther up maybe, but right now we have to leave."

Maniac Man burst out of the crowd screaming at the top of his lungs. "*Polisi. Polisi.*"

His fists raised above his head.

Bima yelled at me, "GET ON!"

I barely had time to sit down. With one arm tight around Little O, I grabbed Zaqi's t-shirt. When Bima punched it into gear, off we roared with Little O's lips popping.

"Little O, we'll be safe. You'll live in the rainforest, green," I whispered into his little ear. "We have to stay on the scooter. I've got you, baby." But with only one hand holding onto Zaqi, who had me?

The scooter at full throttle roared around the corner to escape from Maniac Man, who kept yelling for the police. My butt slid and then my grip on Zaqi's t-shirt loosened. Starting to slip off, when just in time, Zaqi grabbed my arm, pulling it tightly around his body and held it there. Little O's inaugural scooter ride was a nightmare. He flattened against me, wrapped around like a rubber band. His fingers wrapped in my hair, his lips popped loudly, and sending only red, a shower of fear. How could I soothe him now? Certain that the scooter would crash, and scared that I'd lose my grip on Little O, I forced myself to find calm. "Little O, it's me, Jaylynn. Your rescue has begun." *Breathe*, I told myself, *breathe*. "Soon we'll be safe at the rescue center," I cooed. I showed him green and yellow and then more green.

Little O responded with red. A waterfall of fear cascading down.

What in the world was I thinking? Terrifying him on this scooter. And what if we arrived there and he hated it?

Becaks, buses, taxis, and chaos cracked me out of my worries and back to the moment. I held on tight, imagining the rainforest, where his dream auntie had taken me. In a matter of hours, we be at Batu Mbelin. Little O would be home, forever free. I hoped.

After three perfect turns, the fourth one came up too fast.

Bima screamed out, "I MISS TURN. WE GO BACK! HOLD TIGHT!"

Bima made a U-turn in the middle of traffic. The bike slid into the turn. I held in a scream unwilling to frighten Little O. Zaqi held my arm tightly against him and moved his body with the turn. When we arrived at the missed turn, we all screamed. Maniac Man, on a scooter, was driving straight at us.

"STOP! STOP THEM! THEY STOLE MY MONEY!" he yelled.

People on the sidewalks gawked at us as Maniac Man on his new scooter raced after all of us on Bima's old scooter plus a frightened orangutan.

Swiveling around for a peek, what I saw wasn't good. "He's right there, on our tail," I whispered in Zaqi's ear.

"Do not be afraid. Bima drive fast and strong. We safe."

Little O tucked his head under my chin and I rested my head atop his.

After the fifth turn, we'd hit the straight-away. Bima

183

shouted back to us. "I LEAD MANIAC MAN TO
RESCUE CENTER, BUT NOT LET HIM CATCH US.
I WANT TO TRAP HIM. GET MONEY BACK." Bima
drove fast, checking his rear-view mirror. It seemed like
things were finally going our way as we entered the straight-
away. When I peeked back, Maniac Man was racing after us,
not giving up, but not gaining on us either just like Bima
wanted. But in no time at all, somehow, he caught up and
then pulled alongside of us way too close."HE'S TRYING
TO EDGE US OFF THE ROAD!" I yelled. A crash at this
speed might hurt one of us or worse, Little O. My yelling
frightened Little O, who whimpered loudly and climbed
up my shoulder trying to hide himself in my hair. Afraid of
losing my grip on Little O, I started slipping sideways. "I'm
having a hard time balancing," I wailed. "Little O's on my
head. I can't hold on!"

Bima yelled. "HOLD ON! HOLD ON WITH LEGS!
YOU HAVE TO STAY ON OR ALL OF US BE HURT.
LITTLE O, TOO!"

Zaqi kept telling me, "You can. You are strong. Wani.
Little O needs you."

Little O now had both flattened out on top of my head
using my hair as handles, pulling hard with his fingers and
toes all intertwined in my hair. Every time the scooter leaned
to the left or right, my hair got yanked hard. The red waves
rolled stronger. Poppoppoppoppoppop.

"Ouch, Little O. That really hurts. Come down," I
begged.

In addition to the clamor, the familiar smell of Maniac
Man, who had beaten him so often and killed his mother,

terrified him. A tsunami of red hit me. Time to focus, to stay strong, to help Little O stay calm. Fear wasn't an option.

Yellow didn't help. Green was useless. *Gold. Little O feel it. Gold. Time for all the courage we can muster. I know we can get through this. Trust me, Little O.*

Just then Maniac Man veered so close that I felt certain he'd force us into the ditch. Zaqi whispered to his cousin and Bima nodded in agreement. What were they up to? Bima drove a little farther from the edge and kept a steady speed.

At the exact moment, when the man moved right next to us, within arm's reach, but before he could force us off the road, Zaqi acted. Holding on forcefully to both me and Bima, Zaqi kicked his leg out hard and high. He hit him rock solid right on his hip. Completely shocked, Maniac Man's scooter swerved all over the road and though he tried to keep upright, when he hit a pot hole, his scooter flipped over. That miserable beast of a man crashed hard onto the pavement. Bima and I both cheered.

Bima looked back briefly, grinning. "*Ya! Sepupu*, you do it! You save us!" he screamed.

"That was freakin' awesome! Like where'd you learn that move?" I screeched.

Even Little O seemed a little calmer with the smell of Maniac Man gone. When we'd reached a safe distance, Bima slowed to a stop at the crest of the hill. We each turned back for one last look. Maniac Man clenched his fists in the air, yelling something. But he still hadn't stood up or gotten his scooter upright by the time we made it up and over the next hill.

"I want Maniac Man to follow us to rescue center. Maybe police help."

"How long until we get there?" I asked.

Bima shook his head. "Not know. Maybe soon. Maybe long."

Since none of us had ever been there, we had no idea of the exact location. Only that there was a river in the jungle. We rode quietly for the next ten minutes. What if Maniac Man remounted his scooter and found us? What if this time he made us crash?

Only one of us still made sounds. Poppoppoppoppoppop. The only one who had no idea where we were going? The only one whose life was going to change. Would he like the rescue center? I knew he'd prove a good student. He was plenty smart. Would anyone understand his color talk there? So many questions as we four zoomed along the narrow road.

Even though I knew it was the right road and that we'd be there soon, it seemed like hours and hours on the road.

When Bima saw the sign, *Mbelin Batu*, he shouted, "That's it! Look! We made it."

A smile swept across my face as we turned onto a bumpy gravel driveway descending into the sanctuary. The back of the scooter bounced me like riding a bucking bronco. Each bump pulled us closer to the rescue center. Little O mumped softly. What must he think of The Great Rescue now? We came around a bend and saw a group of buildings. In one building at the far end there was a large cage with shelves and a big tree inside, big ropes hanging down. *So where were the orangutans?*

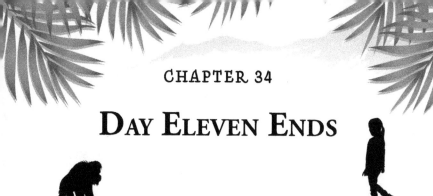

CHAPTER 34

DAY ELEVEN ENDS

Anxious to get both feet firmly planted on the ground, I jumped off first. Little O held me tight with his lips popping continually. "This ride petrified you. Shh, little baby, you'll be okay. Shh…." A back rub was the best I could offer him.

Bima jumped off next, fired up as ever. "Can you believe we escaped Maniac Man? That was a crazy ride. I not believe we made it here. Zaqi, I not know that you have fighter inside. You strong, brave." He wrapped his arm around his cousin, who dismounted the bike slowly.

"He alive? I not hurt him?" Zaqi wore a worried look on his face. "I not hurt anyone but he danger. Had to stop."

"If you didn't stop him, we'd be in the ditch, hurt. You saved us and Little O! He's alive, still yelling with maybe a bruise or two. He deserved that kick. Don't worry." He got a back pat, too. "But now, where are the orangutans? There's no one here."

Bima, not one to worry, looked around. "Come on, you two. Maybe they live in rainforest. Maybe orphans train there. Let's go before Maniac Man finds us!"

We all spun around afraid that Maniac Man followed us. Suddenly, Little O stopped popping his lips and became very still.

"Little O, what's up?" He sniffed the air. "Hey, Little O's acting weird. Does he smell Maniac Man?" I turned again looking through the dense foliage, was he there watching us?

"He know it safe here." Zaqi said. "He know Maniac Man gone."

Bima headed quickly toward a path that lead into the rainforest.

"Hello. *Apa kabar*," I shouted. "Anyone home?" But no one answered. "You're saying we should go into that rainforest? It's really dark in there, like, no light. What if there's something dangerous like a really big snake?"

"Now time be quiet. Listen. Use senses like Little O," Bima said.

The muddy rainforest path slurped with each step. Vines swept across my face like tentacles reminding me of my dreams. Creeping plants hung from the branches. As I crept forward, some low growing plants almost tripped me up. Bima pushed back giant ferns and then Zaqi and I moved fast before they snapped back. The light of day barely filtered through the trees. Small beads of water balanced on delicate leaves. Where were the orangutans?

Little O squeaked out a new sound. Nothing I'd heard before. He scrambled to get down and grabbed a leaf bringing it to his nose to sniff and then gobbled it up. Quickly grabbing more, he moved to the tree trunk peeling back the bark. Instinctively, he pinched a bug between his fingers inspecting it before gulping it down, followed by a noisy slurp.

"Hey, look, you two; he's eating leaves. He remembers." I grinned.

Bima stood silently in the rainforest smiling at Little O. Occasionally his head turned back to where we had parked the scooter. Bima gathered himself to his full height, a fierce expression on his face. Did he think Maniac Man would sneak up on us?

Zaqi reached his hand out toward Little O. "Little O safe. Big Rescue mean he live in rainforest."

Little O finished his exploration and climbed up my leg ready to be held again. With his back legs wrapped around my chest as if I were his mother, he stretched out backwards, arching his back, pointing his chin up, his face looking at the trees. Like a kid at the candy store, his nimble fingers grabbed leaves and stuffed them in his mouth. He stretched out so far, it made all of us laugh. He grabbed something between his thumb and his index finger, twisted his fingers in front of his face, sniffed, and then put his fingers right in front of my nose. My eyes popped out of their sockets as black bugs legs squirmed right under my nose.

"No thanks, Little O. It's all yours."

"Too quiet," Bima said. "Where people? Where orangutans?"

Zaqi shrugged. "We found right place."

The only one, happy to be here and unconcerned, was Little O, who stretched out looking for new bugs and leaves, not a worry in sight. Time for all of us stalled. I worried about this rescue center. If it was safe for Little O, shouldn't people be here? None of us had an answer for the sanctuary that held neither people nor orangutans. It stumped me, but we couldn't go back to Medan.

Little O made the decision for us. Suddenly, he stopped eating and made that sound again. A muumph-ing sound. He grabbed around my head, his face next to mine, then squealed in alarm. He flashed red. I felt his heart beating fast and looked around for Maniac Man.

From deep in the forest, came a mysterious sound. The commotion rumbled louder and closer, making quite a ruckus. Bima swaggered to the front, always the protector. "Jaylynn come between Zaqi and me. We protect you."

Little O responded first with a loud sound, a yell. He patted my shoulder and kept on making the sound. Not able to catch my breath, my heart beat faster as red ran everywhere. We moved instinctively in a circle around Little O.

Suddenly, Maniac Man rushed out of the dense forest screaming at us, waving a big stick. "Give me back my orangutan. You stole him from me." As he came closer, Little O started screaming, climbing on my head and I did everything I could to hold him. Colors were not going to work. He was scared to death of being beaten again, taken away. "Bring him here girl NOW! And then something in Bahasa.

"YOU WILL NEVER GET HIM," I said. "YOU KILLED HIS MOTHER. THE POLICE ARE COMING TO ARREST YOU NOW. DON'T COME ONE STEP CLOSER."

Bima was ferocious. Zaqi looked fierce. But what could

we three kids do against a grown man with an enormous stick. Should I let Little O make a run for it? Or would he even know what to do? He'd never been on his own in the rainforest. What if Maniac Man got ahold of him? And then Maniac Man moved toward us each step bringing him closer making Little O more frantic.

"GIVE ME ORANGUTAN. NOW!"

Bima turned to us and whispered, "As soon as he gets close enough, I'm tackling him. Take the baby and run into the forest. Somehow, I will stop him. And just as Maniac Man took a swing at Bima with his log, we heard a commotion coming from deep in the rainforest. What now? Even Maniac Man stopped. The sounds surrounded us now. Coming closer. Little O beeped wildly and clung to my head, covering my face, wrapping his legs around my neck. Maybe it's like a family of orangutans coming. Maybe they will tackle Maniac Man. For revenge.

Suddenly from the dense bush, a woman burst through the brush holding a baby orangutan, then a man, and another woman holding a baby and another man. "Who are you? Why are you threatening them about that baby? Where you come from?"

Little O stopped fidgeting, staring intently at the other orangutan. Breathing rapidly, alarmed, waves of red descended on me like sheets of rain. How could I guard Little O now? Bima spoke Bahasa to the woman. I watched as all three nodded looking at Little O. I wished that I understood Bahasa. Could we trust these people? Then Maniac Man started ranting about his baby orangutan that was stolen from him. Bima was yelling. Chaos breaking out.

Maniac Man kept coming towards us swinging his stick.

The two men rushed towards Maniac Man, wrenching his stick away, then pinning him to the ground. He kept yelling, screaming in Bahasa, but the men weren't letting him go. They stood him up and started walking him back to the buildings. He kept yelling. The only word I understood was 'orangutan.' As soon as Maniac Man was out of sight and out of smell distance, Little O calmed down.

"Jaylynn, this woman says they will call the police and arrest this man. We can get our money back but even better, she wants Little O to stay here. He will be safe. Learn to swing from vines. She says Little O stay in your arms," Bima told me to follow her to orphans. Learn to swing from vines.

"But I'm worried. Little O's body is maxed out with quivers and shakes." The reality of what would come next hit me. Maybe the red waves were mine. My stomach started doing a nervous dance. *Leave him now? He's my friend. I have to say goodbye? Forever?* Since I first laid eyes on Little O, his freedom had been my only wish. Every ounce of my energy, every minute of my life, spent conniving, plotting his rescue. Not a day passed without focusing on his release back to the rainforest, scheming, and conspiring. My sneaky plot succeeded and now, finally, freedom for Little O.

But that meant that my time with Little O ended here and I wasn't ready. I wasn't happy. I'd never see him again. Not one little hug ever again. No more balloons of yellow surrounding my heart.

"Baby orangutan will be healthy and happy. Only babies live here. Come see them at the forest school," she said.

We followed her deeper into the rainforest, so thick and dark that it could have been twilight, without a glimmer of sunlight or a glimpse of blue sky. My eyes penetrated through the haze, as a blanket of mist engulfed me. Little O grabbed leaves as we walked under the dense forest and made a *grumph* sound that I hadn't heard before.

"Your orangutan is happy when he makes that sound."

Listening to his happy sound, I asked, "What do you think? Is it safe here?" Zaqi shrugged, the look in his eyes full of questions and hesitation, but Bima answered with confidence. "We wait to see, but I think good."

When we got to the forest school, all three of us stood frozen in amazement. An orangutan jungle gym, nothing like any of us had imagined. Leather ropes strung between the trees, low platforms built off the ground and even wire nests hung from the trees, but that wasn't what stopped us cold. This rainforest jungle gym was packed full of baby orangutans!

Inspecting the area, I looked for clues of foul play, for anything that might harm Little O. But the carers cuddled the orphans like nurses in an infant ward. I concentrated on the babies as they learned to swing on vines. *Focus on the good. This place is safe.* Baby orangutans swung happily, hung upside down, and dangled in the air. Lots of caring here, but I had to be certain before I'd leave Little O.

"What? That's crazy! Look at all these babies! Like Little O! I never thought what it would be like here. It's like a nursery! There must be, like, twenty babies, all so happy. Some like to cuddle, like Little O."

Zaqi giggled. "Look at those two. They climb all over

each other. Look fun. *Ya?* Little O free! We did it! He live in rainforest like orangutan. No chain. No Maniac Man. We did it!" Zaqi threw up his hands, smiled a giant smile and then crossed his arms across his chest. Looking at Zaqi's delight, a weight started to lift off my shoulders.

Bima's somber face surprised me. I figured he'd be proud, happy, too. He watched each orangutan and every adult, not saying a word, no expressions on his face, acting all business like, and hiding his feelings. He loved Little O, too. Wish I knew if he was feeling what I was feeling.

Little O inspected this strange new place with his arms and legs wrapped tightly around me but no red, not afraid. What was he thinking, I wondered?

"Look, that little baby in that woman's arms is drinking out of a bottle. Sweet. Did you see those two babies kiss?" I shook my head in amazement and held Little O tight, rubbing his back, kissing his head, feeling a little overwhelmed by it all.

The woman who had led us here let us take it all in, without speaking, which helped me adjust. Somehow, she knew we were nervous about leaving Little O. Finally, she spoke. "Your baby loves you very much. He holds you like his mother. He trusts you. You've been a good friend. All of you."

"Little O gives me lots of love. I got lucky when I found him," I said.

"The Great Rescue succeeded!" Zaqi raised both fists in the air. "We did it!"

"You three gave him love. Love is a strength. You three saved his life."

"Jaylynn found him. She kept pushing to free him. She never gave up," Bima said, held up his hand for a high five, and we all slapped together.

"Ya, she only think about what best for Little O," Zaqi said. He put his arm around me then, my Sumatran buddy.

"We all did this together. A super good team," I told her. Thankful to have found such good friends, I looked at the woman but didn't know what to say. Some of the dread about leaving Little O was creeping up fast.

None of us said anything except Little O, who made his little *grumph* sound. I wished I was ready to make a happy sound.

"He'll be in quarantine first to guarantee he's healthy. I don't know what he's been eating but here, we feed him fruit and leaves. After that, he'll go to this baby jungle school to learn skills like foraging for food and nest building. He'll be in school until he's three years old and then he'll be released into the wild, if he's ready."

"What if it not ready?" Bima asked.

"He'll stay in school. We want him to live life free in the rainforest but only when his skills bring out his instincts."

I watched a caregiver rub a belly and then tickle an orangutan. Was that a laugh? "I guess these are your cousins, Little O. Do you like them?"

Little O popped his lips in response but not like the terror at the market. He gawked at the other orangutans, observing their every move, making little sounds.

One of the adults shouted from her spot under a long vine. "How did you three kids manage to find a baby? Did your parents drive you here? Tell us your story."

Our story? No words came out of my mouth in reply.

Walking away from Little O? Without turning into a sobbing mess? I felt my throat tighten and I blinked fast to keep tears from falling. I took such a deep breath that if you jumped into it, you'd never get out, but then I remembered that I was different now. Stronger. Like he read my mind, Little O hugged me tightly, wrapping me up in yellow like a Christmas gift.

Little O had no idea how his life would change in Batu Mbelin. I worried that my departure would feel like abandonment to him. Losing another mother? I buried my head in his shoulder. Our time together was ending.

The woman walked over to me as if sensing my sorrow and put one hand on my shoulder and the other on Little O. Yellow...but this yellow came from her? "You sense his colors, *ya?*" she whispered. Our eyes met, her smile gentle, I nodded. "I'd like you to come back here to work with him. Your love is strong. You're strong. Help other babies, too. *Ya?*"

The reality of her words settled in. This woman understood color talk. She had invited me to return, to work with Little O. I turned toward Zaqi and Bima. She read me right again.

"Yes, your friends can come, too."

We stood together, me, Little O, Zaqi, and Bima. Time for freedom. Time for Little O to live his life swinging on vines through the rainforest.

Free.

TEN THINGS YOU CAN DO TO HELP ORANGUTANS

Like Jaylynn discovered, saving an orangutan was easier with her gang. Find your own gang and start making a difference. Good luck!

1. **Get your own gang together and create Orangutan Awareness Week at your school.** Use this website for ideas. www.orangutans.com.au/information/schools-orangutan-awareness-week/

2. **Get your gang together to celebrate International Orangutan Day on August 19.** Plan a Wear Orange event with a 5k walk to bring attention to orangutans and a bake sale to raise money. Use this website for ideas. **www.redapes.org/august-19th-is-international-orangutan-day/**

3. **Join the campaign to end the demand for conflict palm oil.** The Orangutan Alliance No Palm Oil Certification Program is a program for manufacturers and brands, enabling them to use the Orangutan Alliance Palm Oil Free certification trademark to certify that no palm oil or palm oil derivatives are used in their approved consumer products. Go to this website and see how you can help. www.**orangutanalliance.org/certification-program/**

4. **Sign a petition with THE ORANGUTAN ALLIANCE and other consumers who want to end the demand for conflict palm oil.** Add your name to demand big brands develop product and new ingredient solutions that do not include conflict palm oil, harm the environment or endangered species. Use this website. www.**orangutanalliance.org/new-page-1/**

5. **Sign a Rainforest Action Network petition to stop destroying the rainforest**. Use this website. www.act.ran.org/saverainforests?_ ga=2.134790961.1991010436.1546466648-1278794492.1546466648

6. **With your gang's help, start your own petition**. Gather support. Put pressure on the government to pass a law stating that products containing palm oil must be clearly labeled. Write to your local representatives and governor to see what he or she is doing about the unclear labeling. Visit your zoo to learn about their efforts.

7. **Become an activist**. Start your own fundraiser. Call on government officials. Make your voice heard. Need ideas? Use the Defenders of Wildlife's advocate handbook that you can find at **defenders.org/wildlife-advocate-center**.

8. **Spread the Word**. With your newfound knowledge, spread awareness of the issues facing orangutans and the rainforest. The orangutans need you.

If you need some inspiration, here are two articles about campaigns that became successful. One began very small with two young girl scouts fighting for what they believed in and the other was a large campaign by a well-known conservation group.

Two girl scouts fought to get palm oil out of girl scout cookies. Their story is an excellent example of what can be done when young people put their energy into change. **www.speakingchange.org/scouts/**

Greenpeace joined up with activists all over the world and after a yearlong campaign found success. Worldwide 1.3 million people joined their campaign. Read about their success story here. **www.greenpeace.org/international/story/20105/a-breakthrough-were-now-one-step-closer-to-ending-deforestation-for-palm-oil/**

A LIST OF INTERNATIONAL ORGANIZATIONS WORKING TO SAVE ORANGUTANS FROM EXTINCTION

Gather together your friends to help baby orangutans survive. Visit these websites to see what they are doing and how you can help. From Australia to the UK, from Switzerland to the United States, from Borneo to Sumatra, all over the world, supporters of all ages are gathering together to stop the destruction of the rainforest and save the endangered orangutans. Find the group you want to work with and start helping today. Like Jaylynn, Zaqi and Bima do a google search to find more groups.

Sumatran Orangutan Society
www.orangutans-sos.org/

Orangutan Species Survival Plan
www.orangutanssp.org/conservation.html

BOS Australia
www.orangutans.com.au/about-us/

Borneo Orangutan Survival Foundation
www. orangutan.or.id/orangutan/

Orangutan Conservancy
www.orangutan.com/about-us/our-mission/

Orangutan Outreach
www. redapes.org/about-us/

Sumatran Orangutan Conservation Programme
www.sumatranorangutan.org/

Orang Utan Republik Foundation
www.orangutanrepublik.org/about-us/

Center for Great Apes
www.centerforgreatapes.org/who-we-are/

Save the Orangutan
www. savetheorangutan.org/

Orangutan Foundation United Kingdom
www.orangutan.org.uk/

Orangutan Foundation Australia
www. orangutanfoundation.org.au/

International Animal Rescue
www.internationalanimalrescue.org/orangutan-sanctuary?currency=USD

WWF
wwf.panda.org/knowledge_hub/endangered_species/great_apes/orangutans/

Philadelphia zoo
www.philadelphiazoo.org/Save-Wildlife/Our-Projects/Orangutan.htm

Conservation Drones
www. conservationdrones.org/

Greenpeace
www.greenpeace.org

Rainforest Action Network
www.ran.org/

LEARN ABOUT CONFLICT PALM OIL

Learning about palm oil is an important first step in helping orangutans. Conflict Palm Oil production is now one of the world's leading causes of rainforest destruction. Palm oil, which is produced by pressing the fruit of tropical palm trees, is to be found, according to the United Nations Environment Program, in 50 per cent of all products on the shelves of supermarkets. There are at last count over 200 alternate names for palm oil. From detergents and toothpaste, to ice cream, biscuits, margarine and frozen pizzas, if you see "vegetable oil" anywhere on the label, chances are that it is palm oil.

From Palm Oil Investigations,
www.palmoilinvestigations.org
"We must make it clear that all palm oil is not bad, and the issue is not going to go away. We do believe it is important to support ethically produced palm oil. But currently it is impossible to distinguish between the good and the bad. RSPO sustainable palm oil is not working and we cannot in good faith support a certification that is dismally failing. A recent study by Purdue University is extremely concerning regarding RSPO certified sustainable palm oil. Deforestation is found to happen faster in areas certified as "sustainable."

The following websites contain information about palm oil.

www.thenational.ae/lifestyle/comment/palm-oil-what-it-is-why-it-s-killing-our-planet-and-how-to-avoid-it-1.723925

www.act.ran.org/sf20scorecard

www.ran.org/issue/palm_oil/

www.orangutans-sos.org/take-action/learn/palm-oil/

www. palmoilinvestigations.org

www.worldwildlife.org/pages/which-everyday-products-contain-palm-oil

www.deforestationeducation.com/products-that-contain-palm-oil.php

www schusterinstituteinvestigations.org/products-with-palm-oil

ORANGUTAN CONSERVATION LESSON PLANS FOR TEACHERS

The extinction of orangutans is a very real problem that involves the conservation of the rain forest, restricting the worldwide use of unsustainable palm oil, and the illegal pet trade. Your students can learn how to help save orangutans and hopefully like Jaylynn and her gang, discover they can actively fight for what they believe in. The following list of websites is a preliminary collection of lesson plans about orangutans and the rainforest. Many of the groups listed on the previous page also have ideas for use in the classroom to inspire young conservationists. I hope they will be an aid in your classrooms. I am available for author talks by skype or in person or to present an orangutan power point. Contact me at **joycemajor1@hotmail.com**.

www.lessonplanet.com/lesson-plans/orangutan/all

www.study.com/academy/lesson/sumatran-orangutan-habitat-diet.html

www.academia.edu/12035193/Conservation_Educator_Academy_at_the_Simon_Skjodt_International_Orangutan_Center_Developing_Inquiry_Skills_in_K-12_Classrooms

www.fs.usda.gov/detailfull/conservationeducation/educator-toolbox/middle-school/?cid=STELPRDB5057674

www.indianapoliszoo.com/learn-explore/teacher-resources/

www.tes.com/teaching-resource/orangutan-fact-sheet-6055130

www.orangutans-sos.org/take-action/learn/schools-resources/

www.theorangutanproject.org/get-involved/schools/

www.nytimes.com/2017/11/09/learning/lesson-plans/endangered-orangutans-and-the-palm-oil-industry-an-environmental-science-case-study.html

www.superscience.scholastic.com/issues/2015-16/090115/orangutan-rescue.htm

www.natureworkseverywhere.org/asset/resources/BorneoVFTTeachersGuide.pdf

www.thecrunch.wellcome.ac.uk/docs/default-source/resources/8-9-Save-our-home/teacher-notes-saveourhome4f044f1e0c8663e39143ff00009d7e70.pdf?sfvrsn=0

www.au.fsc.org/preview.senior-5-6-lesson-plans.a-1123.pdf

www.teachervision.com/subjects/science/rain-forests

www.ypte.org.uk/lesson-plans/rainforests

www.childdrama.com/rainforest-lessons.html

www.brighthubeducation.com/lesson-plans-grades-1-2/46980-conserving-the-rainforest-lesson-plan/

www.pinterest.com/pinningteacher/rainforest-lesson-plans/

www.ran.org/palm_oil_resources/